"I saved your skin. All you need to do now is say thank you," Mikhail imparted with quiet emphasis.

"I'm not going to thank you for your interference in my life!" Kat snapped back at him, galled by his stinging reminder that he had dug her out from between a rock and a hard place. "I'm here to ask you what you want from me in return."

Without warning, Mikhail laughed, startling her, his lean dark features creasing with genuine amusement. "I'm prepared to make you an offer," Mikhail imparted huskily, dark eyes narrowing to gleaming jet chips of challenge.

"An offer I can't refuse?"

"Agree to spend a month on my yacht with me and at the end of that month I will sign the house back to your sole ownership," Mikhail proposed, absolutely convinced that no matter what she said she would end up with her glorious long legs pinned around his waist, welcoming him into her lithe body. When, after all, had a woman ever said no to him?

A Bride for a BILLIONAIRE

The men who have everything finally meet their match!

The Marshall sisters have carved their own way in the world for as long as they can remember.
So if some arrogant billionaire thinks he can sweep in and whisk them off their stilettos,
he's got another think coming!

It will take more than a private jet and a wallet full of cash to win over these feisty, determined women. Luckily these men enjoy a challenge and have more than their bank accounts going for them!

Read Kat Marshall's story in

A Rich Man's Whim

May 2013

And Sapphire's story in

The Shiekh's Prize

June 2013

Look out for more scandalous Marshall exploits coming soon!

Lynne Graham

A RICH MAN'S WHIM

HARLEQUIN PRESENTS®

Recycling programs
for this product may
not exist in your area.

ISBN-13: 978-0-373-13143-3

A RICH MAN'S WHIM

Copyright © 2013 by Lynne Graham

For questions and comments about the quality of this book, please contact us at CustomerService@Harlequin.com.

Printed in U.S.A.

All about the author…
Lynne Graham

Of Irish/Scottish parentage, **LYNNE GRAHAM** has lived in
Northern Ireland all her life. She has one brother. She grew up in
a seaside village and now lives in a country house surrounded by a
woodland garden, which is wonderfully private.

Lynne met her husband when she was fourteen; they married
after she completed a degree at Edinburgh University. Lynne
wrote her first book at fifteen—it was rejected everywhere. She
started writing again when she was home with her first child.
It took several attempts before she was published, and she has
never forgotten the delight of seeing that book for sale at the local
newsagents.

Lynne always wanted a large family, and she now has five children.
Her eldest, her only natural child, is in her twenties and is a
university graduate. Her other children, who are every bit as
dear to her heart, are adopted: two from Sri Lanka and two from
Guatemala. In Lynne's home, there is a rich and diverse cultural
mix, which adds a whole extra dimension of interest and discovery
to family life.

The family has two pets. Thomas, a very large and affectionate
black cat, bosses the dog and hunts rabbits. The dog is Daisy, an
adorable but not very bright West Highland white terrier, who
loves being chased by the cat. At night, the dog and cat sleep
together in front of the kitchen stove.

Lynne loves gardening and cooking, collects everything from
old toys to rock specimens and is crazy about every aspect of
Christmas.

Other titles by Lynne Graham available in ebook:

Harlequin Presents®

CHAPTER ONE

MIKHAIL KUSNIROVICH, RUSSIAN oil oligarch and much feared business magnate, relaxed his big body back into his leather office chair and surveyed his best friend, Luka Volkov, with astonishment. 'Hiking…*seriously*? That's truly how you want to spend your stag weekend away?'

'Well, we've already had the party and that was a little high octane for me,' Luka confided, his good-natured face tightening with distaste at the memory. Of medium height and stocky build, he was a university lecturer and the much admired author of a recent book on quantum physics.

'You can blame your future brother-in-law for that,' Mikhail reminded him drily, thinking of the lap and pole dancers hired by Peter Gregory for the occasion, women so far removed from his shy academic friend's experience that the arrival of a group of terrorists at the festivities would have been more welcome.

'Peter meant it for the best,' Luka proclaimed, instantly springing to the defence of his bride's obnoxious banker brother.

Mikhail's brow raised, his lean, darkly handsome face grim. 'Even though I warned him that you wouldn't like it?'

Luka reddened. 'He does try; he just doesn't always get it right.'

Mikhail said nothing because he was thinking with regret of how much Luka had changed since he had got engaged to Suzie Gregory. Although the two men had little in common except their Russian heritage, they had been friends since they met at Cambridge University. In those days, Luka would have had no problem declaring that a man as crude, boring and boastful as Peter Gregory was a waste of space. But now Luka could no longer call a spade a spade and always paid subservient regard to his fiancée's feelings. An alpha male to the core, Mikhail gritted his even white teeth in disgust. He would *never* marry. He was never going to change who and what he was to please some woman. The very idea was a challenge for a male raised by a man whose favourite saying had been, 'a chicken is not a bird and a woman is not a person'. The late Leonid Kusnirovich had been fond of reeling that off to inflame the sensibilities of the refined English nanny he had hired to take care of his only son. Sexist, brutal and always insensitive, Leonid had been outraged by the nanny's gentle approach to child rearing and had been afraid that she might turn his son into a wimp. But at the age of thirty there was nothing remotely wimpy about Mikhail's six-foot-five-inch powerfully built frame, his ruthless drive to succeed or his famous appetite for a large and varied diet of women.

'You'd like the Lake District…it's beautiful,' Luka declared.

Mikhail made a massive effort not to look as pained as he felt. 'You want to go hiking in the Lake District? I assumed you were thinking of Siberia—'

'I can't get enough time off work and I'm not sure

I'd be up to the challenge of the elements there,' Luka admitted, patting his slight paunch in apology. 'I'm not half as fit as you are. England in the spring and a gentle workout is more my style. But could you get by *without* your limo, luxury lifestyle and your fleet of minders for a couple of days?'

Mikhail went nowhere without a team of security guards. He frowned, not at the prospect of existing without the luxuries, but at having to convince his protection team that he didn't need them for forty eight hours. Stas, his highly protective head of security, had been taking care of Mikhail since he was a little boy. 'Of course, I can do it,' he responded with innate assurance. 'And a little deprivation will do me good.'

'You'll have to leave your collection of cell phones behind as well,' Luka dared.

Mikhail stiffened in dismay. 'But why?'

'You won't stop cutting deals if you still have the phones in tow,' Luka pointed out, well aware of his friend's workaholic ways. 'I don't fancy standing on top of a mountain somewhere shivering while you consider share prices. I know what you're like.'

'If that's really what you want, I'll consider it,' Mikhail conceded grudgingly, knowing he would sooner cut off his right arm than remove himself, even temporarily, from his vast business empire. Even so, although he rarely took time out from work, the concept of even a small physical challenge had considerable appeal for him.

A knock on the door prefaced the appearance of a tall beauty in her twenties with a mane of pale blonde hair. She settled intense bright blue eyes on her employer and said apologetically, 'Your next appointment is waiting, sir.'

'Thank you, Lara. I'll call you when I'm ready.'

Even Luka stared as the PA left the room, her slim hips swaying provocatively in her tight pencil skirt. 'That one looks like last year's Miss World. Are you—?'

Mikhail was amused and his wide sensual mouth quirked. 'Never ever in the office.'

'But she's gorgeous,' Luka commented.

Mikhail smiled. 'Is the reign of Suzie wearing thin?'

Luka flushed. 'Of course not. A man can look without being tempted.'

Mikhail relished the fact that *he* could still look at any woman and be tempted, a much more healthy state of affairs in his opinion than that of his friend, he reflected grimly, for Luka clearly now felt forced to stifle all his natural male inclinations in the holy cause of fidelity. Was his old friend so certain that he had found everlasting love? Or should Mikhail make use of their hiking trip to check that Luka was still as keen to make the sacrifices necessary to become a husband? Had Luka's awareness of Lara's attractions been a hint that he was no longer quite so committed to his future bride? *Forsaking all others…in sickness and in health*? Not for the first time, Mikhail barely repressed a shudder of revulsion, convinced that it was unnatural and unmanly to want to make such promises to any woman, and as for the what's-mine-is-yours agenda that went with it—he would sooner set fire to his billions than place himself in a financially vulnerable position.

Kat tensed in dismay as the sound of the post van crunching across gravel reached her ears. Her sister, Emmie, had come home late and unexpectedly the night before and she didn't want her wakened by the doorbell. Hastily setting down the quilt she was stitching, she flexed stiff fingers and hurried to the front door. Her stomach hollowed in fear of what the postman might be delivering. It was a fear that never left her now, a fear that dominated her every waking hour. But Kat still answered the door with a ready smile on her generous mouth and a friendly word and as she signed for the recorded delivery letter with the awful tell-tale red lettering on the envelope she was proud that she kept her hand steady.

Slowly she retreated back inside the solid stone farmhouse, which she had inherited from her father. Birkside's peaceful setting and beautiful views had struck her as paradise after the rootless, insecure existence she had endured growing up with her mother, Odette. A former top fashion model, Odette had never settled down to live an ordinary life, even after she had children. Kat's father had married her mother before she found fame and the increasingly sophisticated Odette had found the wealthy men she met on her travels far more to her taste than the quiet accountant she had married at too young an age. More than ten years had passed before Odette chose to marry a second time. That marriage had produced twin daughters, Sapphire and Emerald. Odette's final big relationship had been with a South American polo player, who had fathered Kat's youngest sister, Topaz. When Kat was twenty-three years old, her mother had put her three younger daughters into care, pleading that the twins in particular were out of control and at risk. Touched by the girls' distress, Kat had taken on sole responsibility for raising her half-sisters and had set up home with them in the Lake District.

Looking back to those first halcyon days when she had had such high hopes for their fresh start in life now left a bitter taste in Kat's mouth. A deep abiding sense of failure gripped her; she had been so determined to give the girls the secure home and love that she herself had never known as a child. She tore open the letter and read it. Yet another to stuff in the drawer with its equally scary predecessors, she reflected wretchedly. The building society was going to repossess the house while the debt collection agency would send in the bailiffs to recoup what funds they could from the sale of her possessions. She was so deep in debt that she stood to lose absolutely everything right down to the roof over her head. It didn't matter how many hours a day she worked making hand stitched patchwork quilts, only a miracle would dig her out of the deep financial hole she was in.

She had borrowed a small fortune to turn the old farmhouse into a bed and breakfast business. Putting in en suite bathrooms and extending the kitchen and dining area had been unavoidable. The steady stream of guests in the early years had raised Kat's hopes high and she had foolishly taken on more debt, determined to do the very best she could by every one of her sisters. Gradually, however, the flow of guests had died down to a trickle and she had realised too late that the market had changed; many people preferred a cheap hotel or a cosy pub to a B&B. In addition, the house was situated down a long single-track road and too far from civilisation to appeal to many. She had still hoped to get passing trade from day trippers and hill walkers but most of the walkers, she met went home at the end of the day or slept in a tent. The recent recession had made bookings as scarce as hens' teeth.

A tall beautiful blonde in a ratty old robe slowly descended the stairs smothering a yawn. 'That postman makes so much noise,' Emmie complained tartly. 'I suppose you've been up for ages. You always were an early riser.'

Kat resisted the urge to point out that for a long time she had had little choice with three siblings to get off to school every morning and overnight guests to feed; she was too grateful that Emmie seemed chattier than she had been the night before when the taxi dropped her off and she declared that she was too exhausted to do anything other than go straight to bed. During the night, Kat had burned with helpless curiosity because six months earlier Emmie had gone to live with their mother, Odette, in London, determined to get to know the woman she had barely seen since she was twelve years old. Kat had chosen not to interfere. Emmie was, after all, twenty-three years of age. Even so, Kat had still worried a lot about her, knowing that her sister would ultimately discover that the most important person in Odette's life was always Odette and that the older woman had none of the warmth and affection that every child longed to find in a parent.

'Do you want any breakfast?' Kat asked prosaically.

'I'm not hungry,' Emmie replied, sinking down at the kitchen table with a heavy sigh. 'But I wouldn't say no to a cup of tea.'

'I missed you,' Kat confided as she switched on the kettle.

Emmie smiled, long blonde hair tumbling round her lovely face as she sat forward. 'I missed you but I didn't miss my dead-end job at the library or the dreary social life round here. I'm sorry I didn't phone more often though.'

'That's all right.' Kat's emerald green eyes glimmered with fondness, her long russet spiralling curls brushing her cheekbones in stark contrast to her fair skin as she stretched up to a cupboard to extract two beakers. More than ten years older than her sister, Kat was a tall slender woman with beautiful skin, clear eyes and a wide full mouth. 'I guessed you were busy and hoped you were enjoying yourself.'

Without warning, Emmie compressed her mouth and pulled a face. 'Living with Odette was a nightmare,' she admitted abruptly.

'I'm sorry,' Kat remarked gently as she poured the tea.

'You knew it would be like that, didn't you?' Emmie prompted as she accepted the beaker. 'Why on earth didn't you warn me?'

'I thought that as she got older Mum might have mellowed and I didn't want to influence you before you got to know her on your own account,' Kat explained ruefully. 'After all, she could have treated you very differently.'

Emmie snorted and reeled off several incidents that illustrated what she had viewed as her mother's colossal selfishness and Kat made soothing sounds of understanding.

'Well, I'm home to stay for good this time,' her half-sister assured her squarely. 'And I ought to warn you… I'm pregnant—'

'*Pregnant*?' Kat gasped, appalled at that unexpected announcement. 'Please tell me you're joking.'

'I'm pregnant,' Emmie repeated, settling violet-blue eyes on her sister's shocked face. 'I'm sorry but there it is and there's not much I can do about it now—'

'The father?' Kat pressed tautly.

Emmie's face darkened as if Kat had thrown a light switch. 'That's over and I don't want to talk about it.'

Kat struggled to swallow back the many questions brimming on her lips, frightened of saying something that would offend. In truth she had always been more of a mother to her sisters than another sibling and after that announcement she was already wondering painfully where she had gone wrong. 'OK, I can accept that for the moment—'

'But I still *want* this baby,' Emmie proclaimed a touch defiantly.

Still feeling light-headed with shock, Kat sat down opposite her. 'Have you thought about how you're going to manage?'

'Of course, I have. I'll live here with you and help you with the business,' Emmie told her calmly.

'Right now there isn't a business for you to help me with,' Kat admitted awkwardly, knowing she had to give as much of the truth as possible when Emmie was basing her future plans on the guest house doing a healthy trade. 'I haven't had a customer in over a month—'

'It's the wrong time of year—business is sure to pick up by Easter,' Emmie said merrily.

'I doubt it. I'm also in debt to my eyeballs,' Kat confessed reluctantly.

Her sister studied her in astonishment. 'Since when?'

'For ages now. I mean, you must've noticed before you went away that business wasn't exactly brisk,' Kat responded.

'Of course, you borrowed a lot of money to do up the house when we first came here,' Emmie recalled abstractedly.

Kat wished she could have told her sister the whole truth but she didn't want the younger woman to feel guilty. Clearly, Emmie had quite enough to be worrying about in the aftermath of a broken relationship that had left her pregnant. Kat did wonder if some people were born under an unlucky star, for Emmie had suffered a lot of hard knocks in her life, not least the challenge of living in the shadow of the glowing success and fame of her identical twin, who had become an internationally renowned supermodel. Saffy had naturally suffered setbacks too, but not to the extent Emmie had. Moreover, Saffy, the twin two minutes older, had a tough independent streak and a level of cool that the more vulnerable Emmie lacked. Already damaged by her mother's indifferent approach to raising her daughters, Emmie had been hurt in a joy-riding incident when she was twelve and her legs had been badly damaged. Getting her sister upright and out of a wheelchair had been the first step in her recovery but, sadly, a complete recovery had proved impossible. The accident had left Emmie with one leg shorter than the other, an obvious limp and significant scarring, a reality that made it all the harder for Emmie to live side by side with her still physically perfect twin sister. Emmie's misery and the unfortunate comparisons made by insensitive people had caused friction between the two girls and even now, years later, the twins still barely spoke to each other.

Yet, happily, Emmie no longer limped. In a desperate attempt to help her depressed younger sister recover her self-esteem and interest in life, Kat had taken out a large personal loan to pay for a decidedly experimental leg-lengthening operation only available abroad. The surgery had proved to be an amazing success, but it was that particular debt that had mushroomed when Kat found herself unable to keep up the regular repayments, but she would never lay that guilt trip on Emmie's slim shoulders. Even knowing the financial strain it would place on her family, Kat knew she'd do it all over again in a heartbeat. Emmie had needed help and Kat had been willing to move mountains to come to her aid.

'I've got it,' Emmie said suddenly. 'You can sell the land to settle any outstanding bills. I'm surprised you haven't thought of doing that for yourself.'

But Kat had sold the land within a couple of years of settling in the area, reasoning that a decent sum of cash would be of more use to her at the time than the small income that she earned from renting out the land that she had inherited with the house. Raising three girls had unfortunately proved much more expensive than Kat had initially foreseen and there had been all sorts of unanticipated expenses over the years while Odette, who was supposed to pay maintenance towards her daughters' upkeep, had quickly begun skipping payments and had soon ended them altogether. To add to Kat's problems during those years, her youngest sister, Topsy, who was extremely clever, had been badly bullied at school and Kat had only finally managed to solve the problem by sending Topsy away to boarding school. Mercifully, Topsy, now in sixth form, had won a full scholarship and although Kat had then been saved from worrying about how she would keep up the private school fees she had still had to pay for that first year and it had been a tidy sum.

'The land was sold a long time ago,' Kat admitted reluctantly, wanting to be as honest about the facts as she could be. 'And I may well lose the house—'

'My goodness, what have you been spending your money on?' Emmie demanded with a startled look of reproof.

Kat said nothing. There had never been much money to start with and when there had been, there had always been some pressing need to pay it out again. The front door bell chimed and Kat rose eagerly from her seat, keen to escape the interrogation without telling any lies. Naturally Emmie wanted the whole story before she committed herself to moving back in with her sister. But it was early days for such a decision, Kat reminded herself bracingly. Emmie was newly pregnant and a hundred and one things might happen to change the future, not least the reappearance of the father of her child.

Roger Packham, Kat's nearest neighbour and a widower in his forties, greeted Kat with a characteristic nod. 'I'll be bringing you some firewood tomorrow... Will I put it in the usual place?'

'Er...yes. Thank you very much,' Kat said, uncomfortable with his generosity and folding her arms as the bitingly cold wind pierced through her wool sweater like a knife. 'Gosh, it's cold today, Roger.'

'It's blowing from the north,' he told her ponderously, his weathered face wreathed in the gloom that always seemed to be his natural companion. 'There'll be heavy snow by tonight. I hope you're well stocked up with food.'

'I hope you're wrong...about the snow,' Kat commented, shivering again. 'Let me pay you for the wood. I don't feel right accepting it as a gift.'

'There's no call for money to change hands between neighbours,' the farmer told her, a hint of offence in his tone. 'A woman like you living alone up here...I'm glad to help out when I can.'

Kat thanked him again and went back indoors. She caught a glimpse of herself in the hall mirror and saw a harassed, middle-aged woman, who would soon have to start thinking about cutting her long hair. But what would she do with it then? It was too curly and wild to sit in a neat bob. Was she imagining the admiring look in Roger's eyes? Whatever, it embarrassed her. She was thirty-five years old and had often thought that she was a born spinster. It had been a very long time since a man had looked at her with interest: there weren't many in the right age group locally and in any case she only left the house to buy food or deliver her quilts to the gift shop that purchased them from her.

If she was honest, her personal life as such had stopped dead once she took her sisters in to raise them. Her only serious boyfriend had dumped her when she accepted that commitment and in actuality, once she was engulfed in the daily challenge of raising two troubled adolescents and a primary-school genius, she hadn't missed him very much at all. No, that side of things had died a long time ago for Kat without ever really getting going. It struck her as a sad truth that Emmie was already more experienced than she was and she felt ill-qualified to press her sister for details about her child's father that she clearly didn't want to share. Kat knew little about men and even less about intimate relationships.

As she walked back into the kitchen, Emmie was putting away her mobile phone. 'May I borrow the car? Beth's invited me down,' she explained, referring to her former school friend who still lived in the village.

Guessing that Emmie was keen to confide her problems in a friend of her own age, Kat stifled an unfair pang of resentment. 'OK, but Roger said there'll be heavy snow tonight, so you'll need to keep an eye on the weather.'

'If it turns bad, I'll stay over with Beth,' Emmie said cheerfully, already rising from her chair. 'I'll go and get dressed.' In the doorway she hesitated and turned back, a rueful look of apology in her eyes. 'Thanks for not going all judgemental about the baby.'

Kat gave her sister a reassuring hug and then steeled herself to step back. 'But I do *want* you to think carefully about your future. Single parenting is not for everyone.'

'I'm not a kid any more,' Emmie countered defensively. 'I know what I'm doing!'

The sharp rejection of her advice stung, but Kat had to be content, as it appeared to be all the answer she would get to her attempt to make Emmie take a good clear look at her long term future. She suppressed a sigh, for after eleven years of single parenting she knew just how hard it was to go it alone, to have only herself to depend on and never anyone else to fall back on when there was a crisis. And if she lost the house, where would they live? How would she bring in an income? In a rural area there was little spare housing and even fewer jobs available.

Ramming back those negative thoughts and a rising hint of panic, Kat watched the snow begin to fall that afternoon in great fat fluffy flakes. When the world was transformed by a veil of frosted white it made everything look so clean and beautiful but she knew how treacherous the elements could be for the local farmers and their animals and anyone else taken by surprise, for the long-range weather forecast had made no mention of snow.

Emmie rang to say that she was staying the night with Beth. Kat stacked wood by the stove in the living room while the snow fell faster and thicker, swirling in clouds that obscured the view of the hills and drifted in little mounds up against the garden wall. A baby, Kat thought as she worked on her latest quilt, a baby in the family. She had long since accepted that she would never have a child of her own and she smiled at the prospect of a tiny nephew or niece, quelling her worries about their financial survival while dimly recalling her paternal grandmother's much-loved maxim, 'God will provide.'

The bell went at eight and as she started in surprise it was followed by three unnecessarily loud knocks on the front door. Kat darted into the hall where the outside light illuminated three large shapes standing in the small outer porch. Potential guests, she hoped, needing to take shelter from the inclement weather. She opened the door without hesitation and saw two men partially supporting a third and smaller man, balancing awkwardly on one leg.

'This is a guest house, right?' the tall lanky man on the left checked in a decidedly posh English accent, while the very large black-haired male on the right simply emanated impatience.

'Can you put us up for the night?' he said bluntly. My friend has hurt his ankle.'

'Oh dear...' Kat said sympathetically, standing back from the door. 'Come in. You must be frozen through. I've nobody staying at the moment but I do have three en suite rooms available.'

'You will be richly rewarded for looking after us well,' the biggest one growled, his heavy foreign accent unfamiliar to her.

'I look after all my guests well,' Kat told him without hesitation, colliding with startlingly intense dark eyes enhanced by spiky black lashes. He was extremely tall and well built: she had to tip her head back to look at him, something she wasn't accustomed to having to do, being of above average height herself at five feet ten inches tall. He was also, she realised suddenly, quite breathtakingly good-looking with arresting cheekbones, well-defined brows and a strong jawline, an alpha male in every discernible lineament.

He stared down at her fixedly. 'I'm Mikhail Kusnirovich and this is my friend, Luka Volkov, and his fiancée's brother, Peter Gregory.'

Mikhail had never been so struck by a woman at first sight. Spiralling curls the rich dark colour of red maple leaves rioted in an undisciplined torrent round her small face in glorious contrast to porcelain-pale perfect skin with a scattering of freckles over her small nose and eyes as luminous and deep as emeralds. Her mouth was full and pink and unusually luscious, provoking erotic images in his brain of what she might do with those lips. He went instantly hard and his big powerful body stiffened defensively because he was always in full control of his libido and anything less than full control was a weakness in his book.

'Katherine Marshall…but everybody calls me Kat,' she muttered, feeling astonishingly short of breath as she began to turn away on legs that suddenly felt heavy and clumsy. 'Bring your friend into the living room. He can lie on the sofa. If he needs medical attention, I don't know what we'll do because the road's probably impassable—'

'It's only a sprained ankle,' the man called Luka hastened to declare, his accent identical to the larger man's. 'I simply need to get my weight off it.'

Mikhail watched her cross the room, his attention gliding admiringly down over the small firm breasts enhanced by a ribbed black sweater, the tiny waist and the very long sexy legs sheathed in skinny jeans. Aside of the fluffy pink bunny slippers she sported, she was gorgeous, a total stunner, he thought in a daze, disconcerted by the level of his own appreciation.

'What a hottie...' Peter Gregory remarked, predictably following it up with a crude comment about what he would like to do to her that would have had them thrown out had their hostess had the misfortune to overhear him. Mikhail gritted his even white teeth in frustration. So far, Peter's unexpected inclusion in their disastrous weekend of hiking remained the worst aggravation Mikhail had had to bear. Always at his best in a crisis, Mikhail functioned at top speed under stress and enjoyed a challenge. The sudden change in the weather, Luka's fall and losing battle to tolerate the freezing temperatures, their lack of mobile phones and inability to call for help had all played a part in the ruin of their plans, but Mikhail had dealt calmly with those setbacks. In contrast, having to also tolerate Peter Gregory's crassness downright infuriated Mikhail, who had virtually no experience of ever having to put up with anyone or anything he didn't like.

The two men lowered the third to the sofa where he relaxed with a groan of relief. Kat thoughtfully provided Luka with a low stool on which to rest his leg while the tallest man went back out to the porch to retrieve their rucksacks. He returned with a small first aid kit and knelt down to remove his friend's boot, a process accompanied by several strangled groans from the injured man. They conversed in a foreign language that she did not recognise. Without being asked Kat proffered her own first-aid kit, which was better stocked, and he made efficient use of a bandage. Kat then fetched her father's walking stick and helpfully placed it next to them before noticing that Luka was shivering and

dragging a woollen throw off a nearby chair to pass it
to the man tending to him.

'Have you any painkillers?' the hugely tall one,
Mikhail, asked, glancing up at her so that she could
not help but notice that he had the most ridiculously
long, lush black eyelashes she had ever seen on a man.
Eyes of ebony with sable lashes, she thought, startling
herself with that mental flight of fancy.

Her cheeks pink, Kat brought the painkillers with
a glass of water, noticing that the younger posh man
had yet to do anything at all to help. He had also at one
point complained bitterly that the other two men were
no longer speaking English.

'I'd better show you your rooms now. I've got one
downstairs that will suit you best,' she informed Luka
with a reassuring smile, for he was obviously enduring
a fair degree of discomfort.

'I need to get out of these filthy clothes,' Peter Gregory announced, storming upstairs ahead of Kat. 'I want
a shower.'

'Give the water at least thirty minutes to heat,' she
advised.

'You don't have a constant supply of hot water?' he
complained scornfully. 'What kind of guest house is
this?'

'I wasn't expecting guests,' Kat said mildly, showing him into the first available room to get rid of him.
She had dealt with a few difficult customers over the
years and had learned to tune them out and let adverse
comments go over her head. There was no pleasing
some folk.

'Ignore him,' Mikhail Kusnirovich told her smoothly.
'I do…'

The deep vibrations of his accented drawl raised

goose bumps on Kat's skin, made her feel all jumpy and she swung open the door of the next room, eager to return downstairs.

CHAPTER TWO

KAT SCANNED THE messy room she had entered in frank dismay, having totally forgotten that Emmie had slept there the night before and had left the bed unmade and every surface cluttered with her belongings. Unfortunately she had no other room available.

'I forgot that my sister slept here last night. I'll tidy up and change the bed,' she assured Mikhail as she began to snatch up Emmie's possessions in haste, gathering up an armful to carry it across the corridor and deposit it in her own bedroom.

Mikhail wondered why she was so nervous around him. He could feel the nerves leaping off her in invisible sparks, had noticed how she carefully kept a distance between them. No, this was not a woman who was going to butt into his space like so many of her sex tried to do, drawn like magnets to his power and wealth with little understanding of the man who went with those attributes. Yes, he was used to rousing many female reactions—lust, jealousy, greed, anger, possessiveness—but nervousness had never once played a part and was novel enough to attract his attention. It amused him that she had not the slightest idea who he was: he had noticed her total lack of recognition of his name when he introduced himself. But then why should a woman who lived in the backend of nowhere know who he was? That sense of anonymity was strangely welcome to the son of a billionaire who had never known a way of life that did not classify as A-list and exclusive.

Kat returned for a second bundle of her sister's belongings. Mikhail tossed her a bra that was dangling from the lampshade by the bed. Kat flushed to the roots of her hair, feeling embarrassingly like a shocked maiden aunt, and sped back across the corridor, pausing on her return trip to grab fresh bedding from the laundry press. She was so self-conscious when she walked back into the room that she couldn't bring herself to look at him. 'Are you and your friends on holiday here?' she enquired stiltedly to try and fill the dragging silence.

'A weekend break from London,' he advanced wryly.

'Is that where you live?' she prompted, allowing herself a quick upward glance in his direction as she began stripping the double bed, already reckoning that it would be a few inches too short for him and then forgetting the fact entirely as her gaze locked onto him like a guided missile that was out of her control. Her regard clung to the stunning symmetry of his features, collided with eyes that glittered like black diamonds and it was as if her mind blew a fuse. Next thing she was remembering that symmetry was supposed to be the most powerful component in the definition of true beauty…and he had it in spades with his exotic cheekbones, perfect nose and wide, wondrously sensual mouth. She was staring and she couldn't stop staring and the knowledge sent a shard of pure panic through her because she didn't know what was the matter with her.

'*Da*…yes,' he qualified in husky English. 'Luka and I are Russian.'

Suddenly released from her paralysis while he blinked, her face hot and red with chagrin, she fought with the bottom sheet, spreading it, tucking it in, wishing he were the kind of guy who would offer to help so that she could do the job more quickly. But judging by his arrogant stance as he watched from by the window, he had probably never made a bed in his life.

Mikhail dug his hands into the pockets of his trousers to conceal his erection. He was hugely aroused. She was bending over right in front of him, showing off a perfect heart-shaped bottom and the shapely length of her slender thighs as she stretched energetically across the mattress. He was picturing those legs wrapped round his waist, urging him on as he rode her, and perspiration dampened his upper lip, sent his temperature rocketing. He felt like a man who had been deprived of sex for years, and as that was far from true, he could only marvel at the wildly exciting effect she had on him. Thankfully she had stared back at him with a look he knew all too well on a female face: an openly acquisitive look of longing and hunger. Satisfaction gripped him. She wore no rings and she was clearly available...

Having dealt with the pillows in a silence that threatened to suffocate her, Kat glanced at him again, feeling as awkward as a schoolgirl, knowing she ought to be chatting the way she usually did with guests. Except normal behaviour was impossible around him and she cringed that even at her age she could still be so vulnerable. His expressive mouth quirked with sudden humour and she blushed again and tore her attention from him, thoroughly ashamed of herself. She might not be a naive teenager any more but she was acting like one. That near smile, though, had lightened his darkly handsome features, which in repose had a grim, brooding quality, and her heart had leapt inside her like a startled deer; she was seeing another layer of him and greedy to see more.

'Can you provide food for us this evening?' Mikhail asked levelly, watching her slot the duvet into the cover with frantic hands. She was nervous, clumsy, and agitated and it was astonishing how much he enjoyed seeing that rare vulnerability in this particular woman. She had no sophisticated front to hide behind. He believed he could read her like a book and he relished the idea. She wouldn't be that experienced, he guessed, wondering why that thought didn't put him off because he was accustomed to women who were more likely to introduce *him* to new techniques in the bedroom, women as practised as whores but a good deal less honest in the impression they liked to make.

Kat turned her head, glossy russet curls flowing back over a slim shoulder, and refused to look directly at him, focusing on his flat midriff instead. 'Yes, but it won't be fancy food, it will be plain.'

'We're so hungry it won't matter.'

She shook out the duvet, hurried into the bathroom to check it, gathering up her sister's toiletries to tip them into a bag and snatch up the used towels. 'I'll come back up and clean it,' she said, crossing the bedroom.

But Mikhail wanted to keep her with him. He spread out an Ordnance Survey map on the top of the dressing table. The *dusty* dressing table, Kat noticed in consternation, shocked by how much she had neglected her once thorough cleaning routine since guest numbers dwindled and daily financial stress took its place.

'Could you show me where this house is?' he asked although he knew perfectly well. 'I want to work out how far we are from our four-wheel-drive...'

'Give me a minute,' Kat urged, leaving the room to dump the remains of her sister's belongings and extract clean towels from the laundry press. Drawing in a deep steadying breath, she settled the fresh towels on the bed and returned to his side. He was uncomfortably close: she could feel the heat emanating from his lean, powerful body, hear the even rasp of his breathing and smell a hint of cologne overlying an outdoorsy male scent. It was a wickedly intimate experience for a woman who had long since closed the door on such physical awareness around men and it made her every treacherous sense sing. Her body quickened as though he had touched her, a chain reaction running from the sudden heaviness of her breasts to the clenching sensation low in her belly.

With fierce force of will she stabbed a finger down on the map, for she had often studied maps with walking guests to offer them advice on the best routes and view points. 'We're right *here*...'

His hand covered hers where it rested on the map, warm, strong, ensnaring, a thumb lightly enclosing and massaging her wrist as though to soothe the wild pulse beating there. 'You're trembling,' Mikhail murmured in a roughened undertone, using his other hand to turn her round to face him, long fingers firm on her slight shoulder.

'Must be c-cold...' Kat said jerkily, terrified that she was guilty of encouraging a complete stranger to touch her and shocked that she was allowing it to happen. He could hardly have failed to notice her staring, but she was convinced that a male with his stunning looks had to be used to that kind of attention. In a minute he would surely be laughing at her shaking and stuttering like an old maid afraid of her own shadow in his presence.

And it was that last thought, that terror that he had to be seeing her as a figure of fun, that made her compose herself and lift her head high in a determined display of control. It was a mistake for he was gazing down at her, black eyes blazing like fireworks flaring against the night sky, utterly riveting, utterly inescapable. Her throat tightened, her breath entrapped there and a shot of pure driving heat raced through her tall slender body like a living flame. Cold was the very last thing she was feeling, but then she had never before felt anything quite that painfully intense. It was as if time stopped and in the interim he lifted his hand from her shoulder to trace the plump pink line of her lower lip with the tip of a long forefinger and her entire skin surface tightened over her bones in response.

'I want to kiss you, *milaya moya*,' he breathed thickly.

And his words freed her as nothing else could have done, so lost was she in what she was experiencing while she also tried to withstand the hurricane force of his strong personality. She reeled back in sudden shock from him, seriously alarmed by her loss of control and common sense, no matter how brief that moment had been. 'No…absolutely not,' she framed jaggedly, her heart still accelerating like a racing car while his face hardened and his black-diamond eyes turned to crystalline black ice instead. 'For goodness' sake, I don't even know you– '

'I don't usually ask for permission to kiss a woman,' Mikhail retorted with chilling cool. 'But you should be more careful—'

Suddenly the tables were being turned with a vengeance on Kat and she was hopelessly unprepared for the tactic. 'I beg your pardon? *I* should be more careful?' she gasped blankly.

'It's obvious that you're attracted to me,' Mikhail countered with a rock-solid assurance that glued Kat's tongue to the roof of her mouth in sheer horror. 'I saw that and reacted to it... You're a very beautiful woman.'

The humiliation he inflicted with that first sentence was enough to burn Kat up from inside out with shame. So, it was *her* fault he had made a pass at her? That was certainly putting a new spin on an unwelcome approach from a man. He was quick of tongue and even faster to take advantage, she registered with seething resentment. As for that old flannel he had tossed in about her being a 'very beautiful' woman... Who did he think he was kidding? Did she look as if she had been born yesterday? Was that piece of outrageous flattery supposed to mollify her and remove her embarrassment? Furious as she was, Kat clenched her teeth together tight because in some remote corner of her brain she was very much afraid that in some mysterious way she *had* encouraged his advances and that he might have a right to reproach her for the mistaken impression she had evidently given him.

Kat hurriedly shut down her troubled thoughts in the brooding silence; her most pressing desire was to escape the scene of her apparent crime. 'I need to cook,' she said succinctly like an automaton and, spinning round, she walked straight out of the room.

I need to cook? Mikhail was as astounded by that unfathomable declaration as he had been moments earlier when she had backed away from him as though a desire to kiss her were the equivalent of an assault.

He *knew* women—he knew women well enough not to make a move on an uninterested one, he reflected angrily. What the hell was she playing at? Was this stop-start nonsense her idea of flirtation? Was he supposed to want her more because she held him at arm's length? He swore long and low in Russian, still taken aback by what had happened: the absurd and unthinkable, the impossible. For the first time in Mikhail's adult life a woman had rejected him.

Kat dug meat out of the freezer and set about defrosting it. A basic beef stew was the best she could offer her guests. She still hadn't cleaned *his* bathroom but no way was she going back up there to face him again! It was not that she was scared—she was simply dying a thousand deaths of embarrassment with that accusation still ringing in her ears. *It's obvious that you're attracted to me.* The wretched man had turned her knowledge of herself upside down and inside out within the space of an hour. For the first time in more years than she cared to count she had been attracted to a man. He was right on that score; she certainly couldn't deny it to herself. But the last time she had reacted to a man that way she was working as a conservation trainee in a London museum, light years back in her past when she had still been young and full of dreams, hopes and ambitions. And even then, even when she had got all silly and tingly about Steve, her one-time boyfriend, it had not hit her anything like as hard as the explosive effect of Mikhail Kusnirovich had! No, back in those days in a similar situation she had still found it possible to act normally and not like a brainless idiot!

But my goodness, how had *he* known how she felt?

How had she shown herself up? Her ignorance of what might have betrayed her infuriated her, making her feel suddenly like a child in an intimidatingly adult world. It *must* have been the way she looked at him, so she would make sure not to look at him again, not to speak to him, not to do anything that might be misinterpreted. The sheer shock value of having such responses roused in her again would have been quite sufficient for her to handle. She had not needed to find herself trapped below the same roof as the man as well! So, she was not too old to react like that, not past those hormonal urges in the way she had blithely assumed. Well, that didn't make her feel one bit better. And where did he get off calling her beautiful? Did he think she was stupid as well as a slut? After all, only a slut would be kissing a complete stranger within an hour of meeting him for the first time!

A knock sounded and she glanced up from her task of angrily slicing vegetables and blinked at the sight of Luka standing there in the doorway, leaning heavily on the stick she had given him. She had totally forgotten the poor man was in the house!

'Sorry to interrupt but—'

'No, I'm sorry…I forgot to show you to your room,' Kat said for him while she washed and dried her hands.

'I fell asleep in the chair,' Luka told her wryly as he shuffled along beside her. 'Never been so tired in my life yet Mikhail didn't even break a sweat when he was virtually carrying me the last mile. I can't believe this weekend was *my* idea…'

'Accidents happen, no matter how careful you are,' Kat told him soothingly while she gathered up the only remaining rucksack in the hall for him on her way past and opened the door to the room he was to occupy.

* * *

There was an atmosphere at the dining table no matter how hard Kat strove to ignore it. There might as well have been a giant black hole cocooning the chair in which Mikhail sat, for Kat refused to acknowledge his presence. The men ate hungrily and with pleasure and when she served up apple tart and ice cream for the dessert, the compliments came thick and fast.

She could cook like a dream. Mikhail, who had never thought about such a talent before, was reluctantly impressed, although he was anything but impressed to find himself eating in a kitchen. Nor was he enamoured of the childish manner in which she was treating him, although it gave him every opportunity to examine her and admire the way her bright hair glimmered below the lights with her every mercurial movement, note the elegance of her pale slender hands as she shifted them and the dainty silence of her table manners. More and more the depth of his interest in her irritated him for it was not his style. Indeed a volcanic growl of frustration began to swell in his chest when she dared to enjoy a light-hearted conversation with Luka.

'What are you doing living all the way out here alone?' Peter Gregory interrupted to ask Kat abruptly. 'Are you a widow?'

'I've never been married,' Kat replied evenly, all too accustomed to being asked that kind of question by her guests. 'My father left me this house and turning it into a guest house made sense at the time.'

'So, is there a man in your life?' Peter prompted with an assessing, too familiar look that she didn't appreciate, particularly not now that Mikhail had put her on her guard.

'I think that's my business,' Kat countered, feeling that politeness only went so far.

Another man? Why hadn't that possibility occurred to him? She might be attracted to him but she had backed off because she had someone else in her life, Mikhail reflected in an increasingly aggressive mood that was steadily beginning to knock him off balance. He felt angry, edgy, quite unlike himself, his vibrant energy too confined by the walls threatening to close up around him. Being cooped up was giving him cabin fever, he decided broodingly. He had always taken his space, his privacy and his complete freedom for granted. In a sudden movement he plunged upright.

'I'll walk back to the car and collect our phones. Leaving them behind wasn't such a good idea, Luka,' he told his friend shortly.

Kat blinked in astonishment at that declaration.

'You can't go back out there,' Luka objected in dismay. 'There's a blizzard blowing and the car's miles away.'

'I would have returned to it earlier if you hadn't been hurt,' Mikhail replied drily.

'I'd really like my phone back,' Peter Gregory said cheerfully.

Kat turned her attention to Mikhail for the first time since he had entered the kitchen. It had taken considerable control to stave off her insatiable need to look at him again but genuine concern now gripped her. After an instant of hesitation, which gave him time to don his waterproof jacket in the hall and open the front door, she jumped up and chased after him.

The snow was falling thick and fast, the road beyond her gates so deeply engulfed with furrowed drifts of snow that she could no longer see it. A split second before Mikhail stepped off the doorstep with the casual confidence of a male about to go for a stroll in a sunlit park, she shot out her hand and closed it around his arm to stop him. 'Don't be an idiot!' she exclaimed, shivering violently in the freezing air. 'Nobody risks their life to go and collect phones—'

'Don't call me an idiot,' Mikhail growled in rampant disbelief at her interference, his handsome features clenched with derisive incredulity. 'And don't be a drama queen…I am not risking my life if I choose to take a walk in little more than a foot of snow—'

'Well, if I didn't have a conscience I'd be happy to leave you to die of frostbite and exposure in a drift somewhere down the road!' Kat let fly back at him, her temper breaking through. Of all the stupid male macho idiots she had ever met, he surely took the biscuit.

'I am not about to die,' Mikhail fielded with sardonic bite, black eyes full of arrogant scorn. 'I am wearing protective clothing. I am very fit and I know exactly what I'm doing in such terrain and weather—'

'I'm afraid that's not a very convincing claim coming from a guy who had to have *me* show him where this house was on the map!' Kat whipped back at him without an ounce of hesitation. 'Use the landline here and be sensible.'

Mikhail gritted his perfect white teeth, caught out by the reminder of the little game he had played with her. He gazed down at her in furious frustration, her bossiness an unwelcome surprise. She was virtually shouting at him as well and that was a novelty he had never met with before and liked even less in a woman. But her green eyes still gleamed like the richest emeralds in her heart-shaped face while the breeze whipped her torrent of curls round her narrow shoulders and made of skim her pale cheeks. She provided an alluring vision, even for a male who had long since decided that, like children, he pretty much preferred women to be seen and not heard. And that fast Mikhail switched from wanting her silence into an infinitely more intoxicating mood, all conscious thought suspended while his body thrummed taut with powerful sexual need and tension.

Later, Kat would tell herself that he behaved like a caveman and that the way she found herself staring up at him had nothing to do with the manner in which, black predatory eyes glittering, he hauled her up against him with alarmingly strong arms and kissed her. And then the memory of what happened next went completely hazy because she fell into that kiss and almost drowned in the overpowering onslaught of the hungry passion he unleashed. Full of virile masculine power and devouring demand, his hard lips captured hers and thrust them fiercely apart so that he could penetrate the tender interior with his tongue and with a shockingly erotic thoroughness that racked her slender body against his with a helpless shudder of response. All control vanquished, she let the excitement rage over her and through her, tightening her nipples into bullet points, while flashing a jolting sensual wake-up call to her core. She shook in reaction, icy snowflakes melting on her cheeks in contrast to the smoulderingly hot burn of his carnal mouth on hers. It was a connection she had never made before and it was inexplicably and all at once wonderful, magical and terrifying.

'I'll be a couple of hours, *milaya moya*,' Mikhail imparted thickly, staring down into her dazed face with the strongest sense of satisfaction he had experienced in a long time because she was finally behaving the way he wanted her to. 'May I hope that you'll wait up for my return?'

And just as quickly, in receipt of that manipulative invitation that naive sense of wonder and magic that had briefly transformed Kat into a woman she didn't recognise shrivelled up and died right there and then on the doorstep.

'Not unless you've got a death wish,' Kat countered tartly, rubbing at her swollen lips with the back of her hand as though he had soiled her in some way, making his stunning dark eyes blaze like fireworks all over again above her head. 'When I say no, Mr Whoever-you-are, I *mean* it and the answer hasn't changed—'

'You're a very strange woman,' Mikhail gritted, outraged by her and yet curiously drawn by the challenge of her defiance.

'Because I'm not saying what you want to hear? Well, do I have news for you?' Kat told him angrily. 'I'm not the Sleeping Beauty and you're not my prince, so the kiss was a waste of effort!'

Kat watched him stride off in the snow and she stalked back into the house and shut the door with the suggestion of a slam. Wretched, stubborn, *stupid* man! She turned and saw Luka staring at her wide-eyed from the lounge doorway as if she were an even stranger creature than his friend. His mouth curved with sudden unmistakable amusement. 'Mikhail has done trekking in the Arctic and in Siberia,' he delivered in a I-know-this-is-going-to-embarrass-you tone of apology.

Freakin' typical, Kat thought tempestuously, her face colouring at the information: macho man had genuine grounds to believe that he was a superior being in the fitness field. *The Arctic*? Wincing, she went back into the kitchen to tidy up. That kiss? Her first in over ten years? No way was she going to think about that for even ten seconds! That would be awarding the Russian the kind of importance that he already so clearly believed to be his due and she had more backbone than that!

While Kat cleared the dishes from the kitchen table, Peter Gregory talked continuously about his big city apartment and the size of his last whopping banking bonus while dropping the names of several well-known clients, which she vaguely recognised from magazines. Grudgingly she conceded that he was so conceited that he made Mikhail look and sound positively humble.

CHAPTER THREE

KAT WAS PEERING round her bedroom curtain when she finally saw Mikhail returning, ploughing through the snow with his long powerful stride. He was *safe*. She had not been able to sleep for worrying about him and now, although she no longer had an acceptable reason to hover or pry, she very quietly opened her bedroom door to listen to the voices drifting upstairs from the hall below.

'We'll be back in London by lunchtime,' Luka was saying with satisfaction.

'Are you sure you want to leave so soon, Mikhail?' Peter Gregory enquired in a salacious tone of amusement. 'Isn't our hostess hottie waiting up for you? Bet you five grand you can't get her into bed before tomorrow!'

Wishing she hadn't chosen to eavesdrop, Kat turned paper pale and her stomach lurched. In haste, she closed her bedroom door softly shut, afraid that the smallest sign that she was still awake might be taken as proof of some sleazy invitation. There was no doubt about it: men could think, talk and behave like repellent beasts, she thought in disgust. Peter Gregory and his dirty mind certainly fitted into that category. Were the three men really agreeing a bet on the odds of her sleeping with

Mikhail tonight? Clearly that kiss had been witnessed and misunderstood. A rolling riptide of shame and mortification assailed Kat. She had never been more aware of how inexperienced she was in the field of sex. A truly confident woman would have overheard that bet being proposed and sauntered downstairs to make a smart comment that would deflate Peter's ego and show how little she cared for such coarse sexist nonsense. But Kat just felt hurt and humiliated and, unable to think of a smart comment, she paused only to turn the key in the lock before scrambling into bed.

And that was when she thought about that kiss; the recollection of her foolish surrender to it hit her like a slap in the face. She had *let* him kiss her, hadn't made the slightest attempt to prevent him. Even worse, she had revelled in every insanely exciting second of his mouth on hers. Maybe all the years of self-discipline and repression had left her sex-starved and pitifully vulnerable to such an approach; maybe she was every bit the spinster figure of fun that she had feared she was, she conceded wretchedly. She tensed as she heard a slight noise outside her door, her imagination making an unpleasant deduction as a light knock sounded on her door. She froze in an agony of shame, did nothing, said nothing, her face burning as though it were on fire. It crossed her mind that she was being very heavily punished for allowing a single kiss and that she was old-fashioned and badly out of touch with modern mores not to have appreciated that even that small amount of intimacy had evidently encouraged expectations she would never have dreamt of fulfilling.

The following morning that restive night of self-recrimination and regret had etched shadows below her eyes and left her pale and out of sorts with the world in general. She rose early to prepare the full breakfast her guests would expect. She heard Mikhail's deep drawl before she saw him and busied herself by the stove, the nape of her neck prickling, stark tension leaping through her slim, taut length.

A hand touched her arm and she jerked her head around, colliding with his stunning dark eyes.

'I expected to see you last night,' Mikhail informed her with a candour that disconcerted her.

'Sorry, you lost your bet,' Kat framed with dulcet scorn.

His level black brows pleated and he swung back to her, surprisingly light on his feet for all his size. '*What* bet?' he shot back at her.

Her cheeks flamed. 'I overheard your friend offering you a bet last night—'

'Oh…*that*,' Mikhail breathed with a sardonic tightening of his handsome mouth, his spectacular dark eyes meeting hers without a shade of discomfiture. 'I'm a little too mature to bet on such outcomes.'

Kat glanced past him to note that only Luka was at the table while Peter Gregory was still chatting on his phone in the doorway. Kat moved a step closer to Mikhail and lowered her voice. 'You knocked on my door,' she murmured that dry reminder, pleased that she managed to achieve a tone of complete unconcern.

A sardonic laugh was wrenched from the tall, powerfully built Russian. '*So*?' he challenged. 'What does that have to do with anything?'

Kat dealt him a cold appraisal and without another word whisked the hot plates out of the warming oven in the range to serve the breakfast.

'*Ne ponyal*…I don't get it,' Mikhail extended impatiently, determined to win a response.

Kat planted a rack of toast on the table along with a pot of coffee and stood at the window, watching Roger Packham drive a tractor in the field beyond her garden, only vaguely wondering what he was doing there in the snow while she struggled to keep a hold of her temper. She didn't care whether Mikhail *got* it or not. Thankfully he was leaving and she wouldn't have to see him again and recall how degraded he had made her feel. He had assumed that she was so easily available, so free with her body that she might invite him into her bed within hours of meeting him, and that was an insult. He would have slept with her too, had she been willing, Kat thought grimly, and that told her all that she needed to know about him and his outlook on life. Most probably, he was what Emmie called a 'man whore', the sort of guy who slept around, who probably kept a tally of his sexual scores and prided himself on his high success rate with women.

In the continuing silence, Mikhail ground his teeth together. She infuriated him without even trying. 'I want to see you again,' he said flatly, not an ounce of appeal or gentleness in that statement.

'*No!*' Kat told him sharply, her soft full mouth rounding on the vowel sound in a manner that sent his hormones jumping.

'And that is all you have to say to me?' Mikhail growled, outraged by her attitude, luminous black eyes glittering like falling stars.

'Yes, that is all I have to say to you. I'm not interested,' Kat completed with a little toss of her head that sent her fiery curls snaking round her taut cheekbones.

'Liar,' Mikhail contradicted with complete derision and the thwack-thwack noise of a helicopter coming in low above the house almost drowned him out.

But Kat heard him and squared up to him, antago-nism splintering from her. 'You really do think you're God's gift to the female sex, don't you?' she condemned, her scorn unhidden. 'I'm not interested and I can't wait for you to leave!'

'Never thought I'd see the day that *you* got the brush off,' Peter Gregory murmured somewhere in the back-ground while Luka, glancing in every direction but at Mikhail, urged his future brother-in-law to keep quiet.

In a rush, Kat served the breakfast. Two helicopters were engaged in landing in Roger's field beyond her garden. The older man must have been clearing the snow for them to land. She turned back to discover that Mikhail had still not sat down.

'Eat,' she urged him.

'I'm not hungry,' he breathed curtly, colour scoring his exotic cheekbones to accentuate the clean sculpted lines of his darkly beautiful face.

An unexpected stab of remorse assailed Kat, who wondered if she had been unreasonably outspoken and spiteful. Hadn't she made assumptions about him in the same way she assumed that he had made assumptions about her? What if she was wrong? But she had not been wrong in her conviction that he had knocked on her bedroom door the night before, she reminded herself impatiently, wondering where that inappropriate attack of conscience had come from. Soft pink mantled her cheeks just as a loud series of knocks sounded on the back door. Mikhail opened it and suddenly her kitchen was awash with large men in overcoats all speaking Russian at one and the same time. An older man with greying hair greeted him with perceptible warmth and relief. In the free-for-all of competing male voices, Kat concentrated on offering everyone coffee and biscuits.

Evidently, Mikhail was important enough to have a helicopter sent to pick him up to facilitate his swift return to London. *Two* helicopters? Had he arranged that means of transport the night before? Was he a flash high-earning banker like Peter Gregory? Or some big businessman with more money than sense?

Luka was digging through his pockets to extract money to settle the itemised bill she had left on the table. Mikhail swept the bill up, glanced at it and shot Kat a sardonic look. 'You don't charge enough,' he told her forcefully, digging the bill into his pocket, leaning down to thrust his friend's money back into his hand. He tugged out his own wallet and slapped several banknotes on the table.

'Thanks,' Kat said in a voice that conspicuously lacked gratitude.

Mikhail dealt her a hard-eyed look, his superb dark eyes glittering with hauteur and arrogance. 'I will *not* thank you,' he delivered with succinct bite. 'As yet you have done nothing to please me…not one single thing.'

And she almost burst out laughing because he sounded remarkably like a sultan informing a humble harem girl of his displeasure while cherishing the belief that she would naturally wish to improve on her performance. But when she clashed unwarily with his striking black eyes and the inescapable chill etched there, any sense of amusement vanished and a touch of dismay and foreboding somehow took its place.

The men filed out to head for the gate that still led from her garden to the field and the parked helicopters. Mikhail waited to the last while the older man awaited him just beyond the door. 'I'll be in touch,' he murmured huskily, surveying her downbent coppery head in frustration.

Kat studiously avoided looking at him. 'Don't bother,' she could not resist saying.

'*Look at me*,' Mikhail ground out between clenched teeth.

Against her will, affected more by that tone of command than she expected to be, Kat glanced up. Soft pink flushed her delicate cheekbones while a pulse beat out her nervous tension like a storm warning just above her collarbone. Involuntarily captivated by the brilliance of her green eyes against her pale perfect skin, Mikhail studied her with a frown. He watched the tip of her tongue slide out to moisten her lower lip and he went hard as a rock just imagining even the tip of that tongue on his body. Expelling his breath harshly, he turned his handsome head away.

'I'll be in touch,' he said again in a tone of decided challenge.

Kat closed the door, shutting out the freezing air. As Mikhail reached the boundary of the gate he addressed the older man by his side. 'Katherine Marshall. I want a background check done on her. I want to know everything there is to know about her...'

Stas stiffened. 'Why?' he dared as if he had not noticed that very interesting hostile exchange at the back door.

'I want to teach her some manners,' Mikhail grated with a brooding glance back in the direction of the house. 'She was rude!'

Astonished by that outburst, Stas said nothing. As a rule Mikhail never got worked up over a woman. Indeed his marked indifference to the many women who pursued him and even the chosen few who shared his bed was a legend among his staff and Stas could not begin to imagine what Katherine Marshall could have done to arouse such a strong reaction in his employer.

Kat was grateful to be busy once the helicopters had gone. She stripped the beds and in the act of filling the washing machine found herself pressing the striped sheet that had been on Mikhail's bed to her nose, catching the elusive scent of him from the cotton before she even realised what she was doing. Her face hot, she stuffed the sheet into the machine, poured powder into the dispenser and turned it on. What the heck had he done to her? She had sniffed his sheet... She was acting like a loon! It was as though Mikhail had switched on some physical connection inside her and she couldn't switch it off again. She was embarrassed for herself.

Roger Packham called that afternoon with the firewood he had promised her and she invited him in for a cup of tea. With satisfaction he told her the outrageous sum he had charged to clear the snow for the helicopters to land that morning. 'City boys must make easy money,' he remarked with scorn.

'I was grateful to get three guests out of the snow,' Kat admitted, knowing she would use that money to stock up on food because, with the current state of her finances, getting hold of ready cash was a problem. 'Business has been anything but brisk recently.'

'But it must have been difficult for you to have three strange men staying here,' Roger remarked disapprovingly. 'Very awkward for a woman living on her own.'

'I didn't find it awkward,' Kat lied with a determined smile, keen not to play up to the older man's preferred image of her as a poor, weak little female. 'And Emmie's back from London, so I won't be alone any more. She stayed in the village last night.'

Mikhail was gone and he wouldn't be back. She could bury all those squirming, inappropriate feelings and reactions that he had aroused, forget the mortification they had caused her, forget *him*...

'Don't use it,' Stas advised, sliding the file onto Mikhail's desk. 'You've never been the kind of man who would use this kind of stuff against a woman...'

His appetite whetted by the rare event of Stas coming over all moral and censorious, Mikhail lifted the file and flipped it open. He read the extensive information about Katherine Marshall with keen interest, noted the figures, raised a black brow in surprise and knew exactly where Stas was coming from. She was on the edge of bankruptcy, struggling to hang onto the house, a sitting duck of an easy target. Now he knew why he had never seen a smile on her face. Serious financial problems caused stress and might that explain why she had blown him off that weekend? He knew he could act on such information, employ it like a weapon against her. It was what his father would have done with an unwilling woman. Mikhail's handsome mouth hardened, his eyes darkening, for the most unwilling woman of all had been his own mother, a living doll ultimately broken by his father's rough handling. But he was *not* his father and Katherine Marshall was *not* an unwilling woman, simply a defiant screwed-up one, he mused impatiently.

What was it about her that had kept her image alive for him? He frowned, frustration gripping his big powerful frame, for he was suspicious of anything he didn't immediately understand. Three weeks had passed yet he still thought about her every day, hungering for that elusive image even as more immediately available woman failed to ignite the same urgency. His stubborn desire for Kat Marshall was obsessional and impractical and that he could see that and still feel that way greatly disturbed him. He wanted his head back in a normal place and he didn't believe he could achieve that without seeing her again. But while she might be in debt and he was rich enough to solve her every difficulty, there was still one insurmountable problem on Mikhail's terms: his own unbreakable rule that, no matter what happened, he didn't buy women. Exactly where did that leave him?

The next day, Kat received a devastating letter informing her that her house would be repossessed at the end of the month. As she had received copious warnings on that score it was not a surprise. A week after that, she answered her phone and frowned when her solicitor asked her to come and see him as soon as possible. What more bad news lay in store for her? Mr Green could only want to see her about her financial situation, which he had become aware of some months earlier when she had first approached him for advice. He had urged her to sell up, settle what she could of her debts and start again, but she had been desperate to hang onto the house that still counted very much as home for both her and her sisters. Birkside was their safe place, their security blanket, the place to which all her siblings ran to for cover when life got too tough in the outside world. Once it had worked that magic for Kat as well. Losing the house would be like losing a chunk of herself and now, after months of fruitless anxiety, it was finally happening.

'I received this letter yesterday.' Percy Green extended the single sheet to Kat. 'It contains an extraordinary offer. Mikhail Kusnirovich is willing to settle your outstanding debts in full and buy your home. He is also giving you the chance to remain at Birkside as his tenant—'

Kat had turned pale. 'Mikhail…K…?'

'Kus-niro-vich,' the older man sounded out helpfully. 'I checked him out and I'm afraid I haven't the faintest idea how he became involved in your debt situation. He's an oil billionaire, not a loan shark.'

'B-billionaire?' Kat stammered incredulously. '*Oil*? Mikhail's rich?'

Astonishment made the solicitor stare at her. 'You actually *know* this man—you've met him?'

In some discomfiture, Kat explained briefly how the three men had taken shelter with her in the snow the previous month. 'And you say he's suggesting that he pay off my loans and purchase Birkside? Why on earth would he do something like that?' she whispered shakily.

'A rich man's whim?' Percy Green shook his head slowly, his incomprehension unconcealed. 'From your point of view, it's a miracle and a timely one. Obviously since the repossession order would leave you homeless you'll accept this offer.'

'Obviously,' Kat parroted unevenly.

The letter dug into her bag, Kat drove back to Birkside in a growing stew of incomprehension. Mikhail was richer than sin and she was staggered by the discovery. Mikhail was offering to pay off her debts and buy her house. But why would he do such a thing? What did he want from her in return for such expenditure on her behalf? Wealthy men didn't give their money away or waste it. She wasn't a charitable cause he could claim as a tax deduction either. So, what *was* he after? Was he showing off his power? Punishing her for her rejection? But how could saving her from becoming homeless be considered a punishment?

She called the lawyers' office responsible for sending the letter and requested the phone number she needed to get an appointment with Mikhail. Whoever she was speaking to went all cagey and uninformative until her call was eventually passed on to someone else. Once she had identified herself, the attitude changed and the phone number was finally advanced. But the difficulties she had had getting that number from the legal office were as nothing to the challenge of getting past the secretarial watchdogs who were determined to know her business before even considering her request to see their employer. Hot with chagrin, Kat finally admitted that Mikhail owned her home and that she wanted to discuss the matter with him. She was offered an appointment four days away.

Emmie dropped Kat off at the railroad station and showed little curiosity about her sister's unusual desire to visit London. Kat smothered a yawn on the train, her early start to the day soon making itself felt. Clad in a tailored dark trouser suit that she had last worn to attend a neighbour's funeral, she felt overdressed as well as deeply apprehensive and angry. What was the wretched man playing at? What did he want from her? Surely not the obvious? She could not believe that Mikhail would not have far more exciting sexual options than she could possibly offer.

When she finally reached the reception area on the top floor of the impressive office block that functioned as Mikhail's London base, a dazzling Nordic blonde came to collect her and walk her down a corridor. The blonde's curiosity was unhidden. 'So, you are Katherine

Marshall and Mikhail owns your house,' she remarked rather curtly. 'How did that come about?'

'I haven't a clue,' Kat fielded. 'But I'm here to find out.'

The blonde subjected her to another assessing look, her bright blue eyes cool. 'Don't take too long about it. He has another appointment in ten minutes.'

Kat gritted her teeth on a sharp retort and smoothed anxious hands down over her slim thighs to dry the nervous dampness from her palms. A door swung open in front of her. She passed over the threshold and into bright blinding sunlight that prevented her from seeing anything.

CHAPTER FOUR

MIKHAIL TOOK FULL advantage of the sunlight that blinded her, striding forward to seize the initiative and, in a gesture that disconcerted her, he reached for both her hands. 'Kat…it's good to see you here, *milaya moya…*'

He was so tall, so dark and so arrestingly handsome in the sleek formality of a tailored black business suit that he had instant overwhelming impact. Her heart thumping inside her ribcage, Kat gazed up into ravishing dark eyes enhanced by thick black lashes and blinked rapidly, thoroughly disorientated by his unexpected smile of welcome and sudden proximity. A feeling of warmth spread through her, a disturbing sense of security holding her still. In a conscious rejection of that treacherous response, Kat snatched her hands angrily free of his. 'Of course I'm here—what choice did you give me? You're buying my house!'

'It's already done. Technically, I now own a house with a sitting tenant,' Mikhail fielded smoothly. 'A landlord is surely a far less alarming prospect than homelessness and the threat of bailiffs removing your belongings and selling them?'

His reminder of how dire her circumstances had been before he stepped in clamped down like steel girders of restraint on Kat's unruly temper. She was furious with him and deeply resented his interference in her private affairs, but she could not have put her hand on her heart and honestly sworn that she wanted the threat of repossession and the prospect of bailiffs back in her life. In truth it was an enormous relief for her not to be dogged day and night with those fears, afraid to answer the phone in case it was the debt collection agency ringing with demands for repayment, afraid to answer the door bell as well. She breathed in deep and slow to calm herself and reorganise her thoughts.

'Why don't you sit down?' Mikhail indicated a couch in one corner of the vast room. 'I'll order coffee.'

'That's not necessary,' Kat told him, dragging her attention from his bold bronzed profile and energy-zapping presence to examine his office. Large in both size and personality, he had an unnerving ability to utterly dominate his surroundings.

'I decide what's necessary,' Mikhail contradicted and he lifted the phone to order coffee.

Kat had not required that reminder of how domineering he could be and her generous mouth tightened as she sat down on the couch, determined to behave normally and betray no hint of her nervous tension. A wonderfully vibrant abstract painting adorned the far wall, the only splash of colour in a room furnished with cold contemporary steel, leather and glass and everything cutting edge technology had to offer. Mikhail Kusnirovich as her landlord? That was a ridiculous euphemism for him to employ when he had repaid substantial cash sums on her behalf. No longer in debt to the loan company or the building society, Kat now considered herself to be in debt to him instead. Of course, he owed her an explanation for his astonishing intervention.

'Why did you do it?' Kat prompted tautly.

Mikhail compressed his wide sensual mouth and shrugged a broad shoulder. It was not an answer but it was the only one he was prepared to give her. He had no socially acceptable altruistic reason to offer in his own defence. What had driven him had been a great deal more basic and selfish: having seen her vulnerability, he had immediately wanted to ensure that he was the only person with access to it. He was a territorial male and he wanted her more than he had wanted any woman in a long time. And only free of debt could she be free to be with him.

His arrogant dark head turned, his striking deep-set dark eyes winging to her lovely face. He watched her colour beneath his stare, soft pink surging below that pale skin to highlight her bright eyes and taut cheekbones. He liked the fact that she blushed, could not recall ever being with a woman who still had that capability. His keen gaze lingered on her lush pink lips and the shadowy vee of white skin revealed by the neckline of the shirt she wore beneath her jacket. That fast, that easily the pulse at his groin reacted and he wanted to touch her and discover if her skin felt as soft and smooth as it looked. Soon he would know one way or another, he told himself soothingly.

The tension in the atmosphere thrummed through Kat as well. His scrutiny of her lips felt like a physical touch. Recalling the hunger of his mouth on hers, she quivered, her breasts full and heavy inside her bra, the tender tips pinching tight while unwelcome heat surged at the heart of her. With ferocious determination, she reined back that tide of debilitating physical awareness, refusing to be either sidetracked or silenced. 'I asked you why you did it. I mean, you hardly know me,' she continued doggedly. 'It's not normal to go out and dig up a person's debts and offer to settle them. You've put me under a huge sense of obligation to you—'

'That was not my wish,' Mikhail lied, for he liked the fact that he had created a link between them that she could not reject. That he had not given her a choice in the matter didn't bother him because he had protected her home for her when she stood to lose it.

In receipt of that guarded reply, Kat felt her growing sense of frustration surge up another notch and she scrambled upright, her russet-red hair streaming in trailing spirals across her narrow shoulders as she threw them back and straightened her slender spine. Getting an explanation out of him was like trying to pull teeth, she thought in exasperation. 'There's absolutely no point in you telling me that that was not your wish when I'm now in debt to you to the tune of thousands and thousands of pounds!'

'But you're not in debt if I refuse to acknowledge that there *is* a debt requiring repayment,' Mikhail imparted with quiet emphasis. 'I saved your skin. All you need to do now is say thank you.'

'I'm not going to thank you for your interference in my life!' Kat snapped back at him without hesitation, galled by his stinging reminder that he had dug her out from between a rock and a hard place. 'I'm not so stupid that I don't appreciate that if something seems too good to be true, it probably *is*. I'm here to ask you what you want from me in return.'

'Nothing that you're not inclined to give,' Mikhail retorted drily.

Kat was very tense, interpreting that statement in only one way. 'Are you hoping that I will become your lover?' she asked him baldly, lifting her chin as she voiced that embarrassing question.

Without warning, Mikhail laughed, startling her, his lean dark features creasing with genuine amusement. 'Should I not? Like most men, I enjoy female company, nothing more complex.'

That might be so, Kat reasoned, unimpressed, but he had not denied that he had a sexual interest in her. If only he knew, she thought ruefully, if only he knew how inexperienced she was he would probably be a great deal less interested in an era when most men expected women to be equal and adventurous partners between the sheets.

'And I'm prepared to make you an even better offer,' Mikhail imparted huskily, dark eyes narrowing to gleaming jet chips of challenge.

'An offer I can't refuse?' Kat quipped, reckoning that he was finally going to get down and dirty with her and admit what she had suspected all along. He wanted her to sleep with him while pretending that she wasn't just doing it because he had paid off her debts. He was a blackmailer with touchy principles, she thought angrily—in other words a total hypocrite. What bad taste she had in men! How could she possibly be attracted to someone as ruthless as him?

'Agree to spend a month on my yacht with me and at the end of that month I will sign the house back to your sole ownership,' Mikhail proposed in a harsh undertone, for even going that close to his unbreakable rule riled him, reminding him that he had not been himself since he met her. He was *too* hot for her, he decided grimly. It was risky to want a woman as much as he wanted her but it was also exciting to meet with a woman who challenged him, and, while his sane mind told him that no woman could really be worth the amount of time and effort she demanded, it was still the excitement that took precedence every time.

'A month…on your yacht?' Kat repeated dizzily, shaken by the sheer shock value of that suggestion. 'But there's no way I would sleep with you!'

'I find you very attractive and I would be happy to take you to my bed, but I've never forced a woman into anything she doesn't want and I never will. Sex would only feature in the arrangement with your agreement,' Mikhail informed her huskily, his deep dark eyes locked to her startled face with satisfaction. 'I want your companionship for a month, a woman on my arm to act as an escort when I go out and a hostess when I entertain on board.'

Kat could not believe her ears, could not credit that he could offer her the equivalent of a luxury holiday with a big bonus at the end and not demand the assurance of sex in return. She had always assumed that all men wanted sex any way they could get it, but he appeared to be telling her that, if she didn't want to sleep with him, it wouldn't be a deal breaker. 'Why would you make me such an offer?' she pressed.

'If I insisted on including sex in our agreement, it would be sleazy,' he pointed out levelly, loving the way she was still challenging him with her suspicions rather than avidly snatching at his very generous proposition. 'I don't treat women like that.'

'I could do the companionship thing but I would never agree to sleep with you as part of the arrangement,' Kat warned him shakily, her colour high, her level of discomfiture intense. 'I mean that. I wouldn't want any misunderstandings on that score.'

Mikhail said nothing because he could see no advantage to arguing with her. But when all was said and done, the same desire that burned in him burned in her as well. She would sleep with him, *of course* she would, she wouldn't be able to help herself when they were together for hours on end. He was absolutely convinced that no matter what she said she would end up with her glorious long legs pinned round his waist, welcoming him into her lithe body. When, after all, had a woman ever said no to him? Kat had taken fright when he had first approached her in her home, that was all, he reflected wryly, reckoning that he had been too spontaneous and aggressive with her. She would want him to make a fuss of her first and if that was what it would take to win her surrender he was, for once, willing to go that extra mile. The background check he had had done on her had made it clear that it was a long time since she had had a man in her life. Naturally she would have reservations and insecurities. He could even understand that she might be a little shy, but ultimately he believed that she would satisfy his driving need to possess her. Women were invariably flattered rather than repelled by the strength of a man's desire.

The gorgeous blonde who had escorted Kat into Mikhail's office also delivered the coffee, her bright blue eyes skimming left and right with keen curiosity as she picked up on the tension in the room. Stiff with self-consciousness and with her own gaze carefully veiled, Kat lifted the cup and saucer and struggled to sip hot coffee with her throat muscles so tense that she could barely swallow. Intelligence and growing caution warned her not to betray weakness in Mikhail's radius. He would use it against her: he was a ruthless man. In her ignorance weeks earlier, she had had no idea of the extent of Mikhail's power and influence and even less grasp of his inflexible drive. Her rejection had clearly challenged him and dented his pride. What else was she to think? Why else would he have come after her? And he had, without a doubt, come after her all guns blazing, Kat conceded in a daze, still stunned that he had gone to such lengths to exert his dominance over her. Yet he had done so. Having identified her financial vulnerability, he had employed it as a means of bringing her to heel. He owned everything that mattered to her lock, stock and barrel and there was nothing she could do about that.

Well, option one was to walk away, acknowledging that losing her home had been on the cards anyway, Kat reasoned feverishly. That would create a stalemate that would certainly surprise and disappoint Mikhail, but ultimately it would gain Kat nothing. Yet what was the alternative? She had not the slightest desire to play the victim and whinge about his callous blackmailing tactics. On the other hand, Kat thought on a sudden strong surge of adrenalin, if she had the gumption to fight Mikhail on his own playing field and *win* she would have her home as a prize at the end of it all. And wasn't a secure base what she really needed, especially now with Emmie pregnant and both of them currently unemployed? Birkside meant so much more to Kat than mere bricks and mortar. It was in every sense the only home she had ever had and very much at the heart of the family she had created with her sisters. How could they still be a family if she no longer had a home her sisters could visit in times of need?

Mikhail was engaged in a dangerous game of one-upmanship, Kat mused thoughtfully, studying his stunning dark features with innate suspicion from below her lashes, for she recognised that he was a clever, sharp-as-tacks operator. He said he didn't expect sex as part of his arrangement but while Kat might be sexually untried she was no fool. She had read all about Mikhail and his ever-changing harem of readily available women on the Internet. This was a guy who didn't do relationships, he only did *sex*. Mikhail was accustomed to easy conquests seduced by his spectacular dark good looks, incredible wealth and dominant personality. Without a doubt, he was assuming that Kat would be just the same as her predecessors and that secluded with him on his yacht she would ultimately succumb to his undeniable sexual charisma. But in that assessment he was wrong, *very* wrong. Kat, dragged up by a mother who was a pushover for every wealthy man who looked her way, had formed her own very effective defences. She had learnt at too young an age that the average man would promise a woman the moon if he wanted her in his bed badly enough. Time and time again Odette had fallen for such promises only to be betrayed once the man involved gained the intimacy that he craved. For that reason, trusting men had never come naturally to Kat, which was why she was still a virgin at thirty-five. She had always wanted commitment before she put her body on the line. Steven had talked the talk but hadn't stuck around long enough to prove that he could walk the walk as well.

'Share your thoughts with me,' Mikhail urged in the charged silence.

He was a class act, Kat conceded with bitter amusement, stealing a glance at his riveting, darkly beautiful face, lingering on the glittering eyes that added threat and vitality to those lean tough features. Her biggest mistake would be to forget that they were essentially enemies, set as they both were on opposing goals. For one of them to win, the other had to lose and she doubted that Mikhail had much experience of being in the loser's corner or that he would be gracious in defeat. She tilted her chin with determination and said quietly, 'If I was to seriously consider your proposition, I would first need legal guarantees.'

Surprise momentarily assailed Mikhail, who had not anticipated such a cool, rational response from her. 'Guarantees with regard to what?' he queried with complete calm, once again relishing the fact that she could still have the power to disconcert him.

'Primarily a guarantee that regardless of what does or doesn't happen on that yacht of yours, if I put in the required time with you, I still get the house back,' Kat proposed dry-mouthed, knowing that that was the most crucial safeguard she required.

'Of course,' Mikhail conceded, affronted by her terminology, his sculpted jaw line clenching with all-male disdain. He had offered her a month of unimaginable luxury on his yacht, *The Hawk*, an invitation that countless women would kill to receive, and she talked about 'putting in her time' with him as though she were referring to a prison stretch? Even worse, she was questioning his word of honour. 'But I too would expect guarantees...'

Kat dragged in a sustaining breath, almost mesmerised by the intensity of his scrutiny and the slow heavy thud of her heartbeat. Her mouth ran dry, a flock of nervous butterflies unleashing in her tummy and clenching the muscles in her pelvis tight. 'Of what kind?'

'That you would fulfil the role of hostess and companion as directed by me,' Mikhail extended coolly, the beginnings of a smile of satisfaction starting to curl the corners of his expressive mouth. 'I didn't think you would agree to this so easily—'

'Only a fool would look a gift horse in the mouth!' Kat quipped in protest, colour firing her cheeks at the calculating mercenary role she was forcing herself to play, not only to protect herself, but also to grab at the chance to get her much-loved home back. 'You're offering me a month of work to regain ownership of my home. From any angle, that's a golden opportunity for me.'

It was the truth and yet making such a declaration, so clearly motivated by greed, made Kat want to cringe with shame. What on earth was she doing? Hadn't she raised her sisters to put principles and conscience ahead of financial success? Yet had Mikhail not deliberately yoked her to that financial obligation, she would never have thought or acted in such a way. Playing him at his own game was self-defence, nothing more, she told herself uncomfortably. He was only going to get the disappointment he deserved for putting her in such an impossible position in the first place.

Mikhail crushed the disturbing pang of dissatisfaction that her candour awakened in him. After all, he motivated employees with bonuses and thought nothing of the practice. Why should Kat Marshall be any different from all the other women attracted by his great wealth? He was *not* buying her; he was *not* paying for her time…hell, he hadn't even slept with her yet! Suppressing the uneasiness stirring inside him, Mikhail chose to think instead of having her all to himself on *The Hawk,* his ocean-going yacht, and the hunger took over again, wiping away every other thought and impression with startling efficiency.

* * *

That evening, Emmie was thunderstruck when her older sister told her why she had gone to London. While intellectually Emmie knew her sister was a beautiful woman, neither Emmie nor her siblings had ever considered Kat in that light, having always been content to accept their sister's claim that she had moved past the age where she still wanted a man in her life. For that reason she simply could not begin to imagine how Kat's supposed charms could have ignited as much interest in a Russian billionaire as some celebrity sex kitten might have done.

Wide-eyed with shock, she stared at her older sister. 'Are you sure this guy hasn't somehow got you mixed up with Saffy?'

'No, he never mentioned Saffy except to ask why she hadn't helped me with my financial problems.'

Emmie grimaced. 'Because Saffy, our drop-dead perfect supermodel sister, may earn a fortune but she is too selfish to think that her own family might need help more than that African orphan school she supports.'

Kat gave the younger woman a pained appraisal. 'Saffy would have helped if I'd asked but I didn't feel it was her responsibility,' she said awkwardly.

Kat didn't want to admit that since most of the debt had been caused by the cost of Emmie's surgery she had been reluctant to approach Saffy for assistance. Emmie would have felt horribly guilty and Saffy could have reacted with angry resentment and the bad feeling between the twins might well have increased.

Emmie continued to stare at Kat. 'So, this guy will do just about anything to get you onto his yacht?' she prompted, still unflatteringly incredulous at the idea that any man could be attracted to her older sister to that extent. 'Doesn't that scare you?'

Kat resisted a sudden urge to confide that Mikhail's fierce desire for her company had to be the biggest ego boost she had ever experienced, but that was a truth that had only recently occurred to her. Even so it was a fact: no man had ever wanted her that much, certainly not Steve, who had taken fright and bolted the minute she agreed to give a home to her younger sisters.

'It surprises me,' Kat admitted. 'I suspect it has a lot to do with the fact that Mikhail's not used to meeting women who say no.'

'But will he continue to take no for an answer?' Emmie prompted anxiously. 'If you're marooned on some yacht with him, can you trust him to keep his hands to himself?'

Kat's tummy somersaulted as she recalled the flash-fire heat of Mikhail's mouth on hers and the silken tangle of his thick hair between her fingers. Yes, Mikhail would keep his hands to himself as long as she kept her hands off him, which she would, of course she would. His kiss on the doorstep had taken her by surprise. If he touched her again she would be better prepared and ready to deal with that weakening surge of temptation that emptied her mind of all sensible thought. After all, it would be very unfair if she encouraged him without having any intention of ultimately going to bed with him.

'Yes, in that line I do think I can trust him. He's too proud to put pressure on a woman who doesn't want him.'

'But he's still willing to pay richly just for the pleasure of your company?' the younger woman queried distrustfully.

'It's only a job…a stupid macho whim on his part,' Kat argued.

'But you know if you *were* sleeping with him this particular job would bear a close resemblance to prostitution.'

Kat paled. 'I'm not going to sleep with him and I've already warned him about that upfront…'

Emmie grinned at that blunt admission. 'Some men would see that as a challenge.'

'If he does, that's his problem, not mine,' Kat pointed out. 'But what's a month out of my life if it secures this house for us again?'

'I take your point,' Emmie conceded thoughtfully.

'You'll stay on here to look after Topsy when she comes home from school for the Easter holidays?' Kat checked.

'Of course. I've nowhere else to go.' Emmie hesitated. 'Just promise me that you won't go falling for this bloke, Kat.'

'I'm not that much of a fool—'

'You're as soft as butter, you know you are,' Emmie responded ruefully.

But during the following week when Kat learned exactly what was entailed in the role of acting as an escort for a Russian oligarch, she felt anything but as soft as butter. First of all, she sustained a nerve-racking visit from a smooth London lawyer bearing a ten-page document, which he described as 'an employment contract' and which delineated in mind-numbing detail what Mikhail would expect from her: perfect grooming, courtesy and an unstinting readiness to please Mikhail and his guests in her role either as companion or hostess, good timekeeping, minimal use of alcohol and no use whatsoever of drugs. In return for successfully fulfilling those expectations for one calendar month, Birkside would be signed over to her.

The reference to grooming mortified Kat, but on reflection she could not even remember when she had last done her nails, and when Mikhail's PA phoned her to tell her that she had an appointment to keep at a London beauty salon on the same day that she was to present herself for her new role, she saw no good reason to argue. It was all part and parcel of the position she had accepted, she told herself comfortingly, and it was not unreasonable that he should want her to look her best. As her slender wardrobe was in no way up to the challenge of a stay on a luxury yacht, she could only assume that he was planning to take care of that problem as well. Sixth sense warned her that Mikhail Kusnirovich left very little to chance and she wondered what would happen when he finally appreciated that she was not supermodel material and was actually very ordinary. After all, he somehow seemed to have formed an image of her very far removed from reality and clearly imagined that she was more fascinating and desirable than she truly was. When that false impression melted away and he was disappointed would he send her home early? She could not believe that he would seek to retain her presence on his wretched yacht for an entire month. In her own opinion he would quickly get bored with her.

On the same day that Kat was collected off the London train by a car that ferried her to an exclusive beauty salon, Mikhail registered that he was in an unusually good mood. He could not concentrate on business: his mind kept on wandering down undisciplined paths as he wondered which of the many outfits he had personally selected for Kat she would wear that evening to dine with him. Only the nagging reminder that he had virtually *paid* for her presence by dangling that shabby little house on the hillside like a carrot to tempt her took the edge off his anticipation and satisfaction. He looked forward to the day when she would try to cling to him as all women did and he would send her on her way, bored with what she had to offer. His face hardened at that desirable prospect: the day of his indifference would come, it always did. In the end he would discover that she was no different from and no more special than any other woman he had taken to his bed and the kick of lust that even the thought of her roused would die a natural death.

Kat was surprised to discover that she enjoyed the grooming session at the beauty salon, although she was just a little shocked by some of the waxing options she was casually offered. That obstacle overcome, she took pleasure in the new arch in her brows and the pretty pale pink of her perfectly manicured nails, not to mention the silky, glossy shine of her curls once the stylist had finished fussing with her hair. She wasn't terribly keen on the professional make-up session that transformed her face but she tolerated it, noting that it gave her cheekbones she had not known she possessed, rather Gothic dramatic eyes and ruby red lips. She thought she looked a bit like a vampire but assumed it was fashionable and resisted the urge to rub a good half of the cosmetics off again. Presumably this was the look *he* wanted and expected.

The limo delivered her to an opulent city hotel where she was wafted straight up to a spacious suite and shown into a bedroom with closets and drawers already packed with what appeared to be her new wardrobe. She blinked in shock, catching her unfamiliar reflection in a mirror and batting her false eyelashes for effect. A vampire or maybe even that wicked Cruella de Ville character from the Dalmatians book? Keen to embrace a new persona that seemed infinitely more exciting than her more average self, she chose a black lace dress from the packed closet. She was sliding her feet into perilously high red-soled designer shoes, the hem of the dress frothing silkily above her knees, when the phone by the bed buzzed.

'I'm waiting in the lobby for you,' Mikhail told her with audible male impatience roughening his deep dark drawl. 'Didn't you get my message?'

'No, I didn't…I'm sorry!' Kat muttered in a bit of a panic, tossing some essentials into a tiny bag and already hurrying towards the door as she recalled that clause about good timekeeping. He didn't like to be kept waiting. The show, she recognised giddily, was finally going *live*….

CHAPTER FIVE

MIKHAIL SAW KAT step out of the lift. She looked stunning but oddly different in a way he didn't like. His keen gaze narrowed as she moved towards him and he absorbed the theatrical make-up that spoiled the natural quality she had had and which he had not even realised until that moment had made her so appealing to him. His dark brows drew together in a frown of displeasure.

Kat couldn't even breathe when she saw Mikhail staring across the foyer at her, almost six and a half feet of lean powerful male with his arrogant dark head held at an imperious angle. He was shockingly good-looking, spectacularly sexy and the dark masculine intensity of his appraisal sent a shard of high-voltage heat shooting down through her tummy. She swallowed hard, mouth running dry, perspiration dampening her short upper lip, the tiny hairs at the nape of her neck standing erect as a frisson of fierce physical awareness tightened the skin over her bones.

'The car's waiting outside for us,' Mikhail told her as the four men she recognised from their visit to her house closed around them, opening the exit door, checking the street in advance before striding across the pavement to open the passenger door of the waiting limo.

'Are those men security guards?' Kat enquired, sliding along the sumptuously upholstered leather back seat, striving not to gape at the opulent fittings surrounding her.

'*Da*...yes,' Mikhail confirmed. 'Why are you wearing so much make-up?'

That directness of the question startled Kat. She blinked. 'I didn't put it on,' she responded. 'The make-up girl at the beauty place did it—'

'Why did you allow it?'

Her smooth brow creased. 'I didn't know I had a choice. I assumed this was the one-size-fits-all look you like your companions to have.'

His mouth set into a harsh line. 'You are not expected to conform to some ludicrous identikit female appearance for my benefit. I have no such preference. I respect individuality and I expect you to make your own choices about such things. I also liked you the way you were.'

'Understood.' Her generous mouth tilted in amusement at his honesty. He was very blunt but she found that remarkably refreshing in comparison to the polite and often meaningless fictions that people spouted. 'So, I'll take off the false eyelashes the first chance I get. It feels like I'm wearing fly swats on my eyelids.'

Unexpectedly, Mikhail laughed, black eyes gleaming with appreciation as he lounged back in the corner of the limo, long powerful thighs spread in relaxation, and scrutinised her slender figure in the fitted black dress: the small high breasts, the tiny waist and slim shapely knees. Arousal hummed through him. 'Talk to me,' he urged lazily. 'Tell me why you took on responsibility for your half-sisters.'

Naturally Kat had accepted that Mikhail had to know a good deal about her life when he had discovered how much she was in debt, but that question made her green eyes flash with annoyance, for she did not like the idea that she had surrendered the right to all privacy. 'I'm sure you're not really interested.'

'Would I have asked if I wasn't?'

'How would I know?' Kat replied flippantly, shooting him a look of barely concealed resentment. 'It's quite simple. My mother couldn't cope with my sisters and she put them into foster care. They were very unhappy when I visited them and I wanted to help—I was the only person who *could* help.'

'It was a generous act for so young a woman—you sacrificed your freedom—'

'Freedom's not always the gift people like to think it is. Family's important to me and I never really had that security when I was a child. I also wanted my sisters to know that I cared about them,' she admitted grudgingly.

Dense black lashes framed the shrewd gaze still welded to her, his dark eyes lightening with male appreciation. 'Why do you always want to argue with me?'

'Do you want an honest answer?' Kat enquired.

'*Da*,' he confirmed huskily, but in that moment he was mental miles away, engaged in imagining her graceful length adorned with pearls and nothing else. No, not pearls, he decided, rubies or emeralds to enhance that porcelain-pale complexion.

'You're so sure of yourself and so arrogant that you irritate me,' Kat confessed, lush red-tinted lips pouting as she framed the words.

Mikhail's body tensed because he very much wanted to nibble at that full lower lip, but for the first time in his life with a woman he hesitated to do exactly what he wanted. He didn't need to dive at her like a starving man being offered a last meal. He could practise restraint, couldn't he?

'I can't understand why a man acting like a man should irritate you,' Mikhail told her with amusement, his healthy and exuberant ego gloriously impervious to her criticism, for he had never known what it was to doubt that he knew best in every situation. 'Unless you prefer weaklings…in which case I could never hope to please you.'

Involuntarily studying him, taking in the amusement illuminating his dark as night eyes and the tug of a smile pulling at the corner of his stubborn mouth, Kat stiffened, resisting his potent masculine charisma with all her might. Companion, she reminded herself staunchly, not his lover or one of his admirers. 'You do realise that you're going to get bored with me?' she warned him.

'How could you bore me when you're quite unlike any other woman I've met before?' Mikhail countered with lazy assurance. 'I never know what strange thing you will say next, *milaya moya*.'

As Kat was not aware that she had ever said anything that might be considered strange to him she was, not unnaturally, silenced by that statement. The limo drew up in a quiet street and they alighted, Mikhail clamping his big hand to her slim hip to draw her below the shelter of his arm when she would have put greater distance between them. Disturbingly conscious of his proximity and the familiar scent of his cologne, not to mention the weight and position of his hand near her derriere, Kat had to fight the desire to pull away from him, knowing it would be as welcome to him as a slap in the face. She had to be more tolerant and relaxed, she instructed herself sternly. She was a grown woman and there was no need for her to behave like a jumpy teenager around him.

His security team ushered them into a low-lit restaurant. They were greeted at the door by the proprietor, who bowed as low as if royalty had arrived. A sudden hush fell among the other diners and heads swivelled in their direction. Mikhail addressed the proprietor in his own language. They were shown to a table and menus were presented with much bowing and scraping. Yes, it was very like being out in public with royalty, Kat decided ruefully, glancing down at her menu only to discover that it was incomprehensible to her.

'Is this a Russian restaurant?' Kat enquired.

Mikhail nodded calmly. 'I often eat here.'

'The menu's in Russian—I can't read it,' Kat pointed out stiffly a couple of minutes later because he still hadn't noticed that she was having a problem.

'I'll choose for you,' Mikhail announced rather than offering to play translator for her benefit.

Kat gritted her teeth again, wondering how she would get through the month without trying to kill him at least once. He existed in his own little bubble of supreme confidence, King of all he surveyed, blithely, unashamedly selfish and stubborn. *Her* needs, *her* wants did not exist as far as he was concerned. Suddenly she wondered if that meant that he would be rubbish in bed and hot-pink chagrin flooded her complexion at that uncharacteristic thought on her part. As she had no intention of going to bed with him, she would never know the answer to that question, she reminded herself irritably.

'What's wrong?' Mikhail asked, recognising the tension in her fine-boned features while at the same time wishing she would go and wipe off all the metallic grey make-up obscuring her beautiful eyes.

'Nothing…' Kat forced a valiant smile while he ordered their meals in Russian without consulting her preferences or even telling her what he had chosen for her to eat. She was doing this to regain her family home and she could put up with being treated like a piece of inanimate furniture for the sake of the house, she told herself staunchly.

Mikhail signalled Stas and gave him an instruction that startled the older man into glancing in surprise at Kat.

The first course arrived and it was caviar served with strips of hot buttered toast. Kat had never liked fish—in fact even the smell of anything fishy made her tummy roll. Mikhail failed to notice how little she ate and was equally impervious to the fact that she only took a few mouthfuls of the equally fishy soup that followed. Stas then approached her with a package, which he handed to her.

'The make-up…you can remove it now,' Mikhail informed her with satisfaction as she glanced into the bag in disbelief and discovered a pack of wipes.

Taken aback by the request that she remove her make-up while she was out in public, Kat vanished to the cloakroom and carefully peeled off the false eyelashes before wiping off the dramatic eye shadow. The effort left her eyelids slightly swollen, not that she supposed that that little consequence would matter to Mikhail, whose main goal in life always seemed to be getting exactly what he wanted from those around him. He didn't seem to respect or even notice the normal boundaries that other people observed. After only a couple of hours Kat was reeling in shock from the challenge of dealing with such a force of nature. She dug into her bag for her own small stock of cosmetics and applied some foundation and lip gloss to banish the bare look from her face.

'Much better,' Mikhail told her approvingly when she reappeared, looking more as he remembered her. He was as comfortable with her transformation and his determined control of it as she was not. 'I can see *you* again.'

Mercifully, a giant succulent steak arrived for Kat's main course and she was finally able to satisfy her appetite with something she could eat. The dessert was something cheesy covered with honey. After that no-holds-barred introduction to Mikhail's national cuisine, dutifully drinking down the special vodka he praised to the skies and ending on coffee seemed almost tame in comparison.

He then asked her if she wanted to visit a club and Kat felt like a party pooper when she admitted that it had been a long and very busy day and that she was tired.

As they stepped out of the restaurant onto the shadowy street, a dark shape lunged at her without warning and a shocked cry of fear erupted from Kat. Just as abruptly, Mikhail thrust her behind him and stepped between her and her apparent assailant with what sounded very much like an oath. In the scuffle that followed, men seemed to jump from all directions and she fell back into the doorway breathless and full of alarm, her heart thundering in her eardrums as she appreciated that Mikhail already had the man pinned down in a pretty threatening manner. Stas, the head of his security team, was intervening and he and Mikhail momentarily seemed to be engaged in some sort of a dispute. Mikhail's anger was audible in his dark deep voice. Shaking the terrified-looking man he still held as a terrier might shake a rat, Mikhail released him with a sound of disgust and swung round to retrieve Kat.

'Are you all right?' Mikhail demanded thunderously.

'I got a fright…that's all,' Kat framed shakily.

'I saw the street light gleam on something in his hand—I thought he had a knife,' Mikhail grated, shepherding her with determination towards the limo where the passenger door already stood open. 'But it was just a camera—he's only an idiot paparazzo trying to steal a photo!'

Still trembling from the shock of the incident, Kat settled into the passenger seat and marvelled at the way in which her attitude to Mikhail Kusnirovich had been turned on its head within the space of a minute. He might have neglected to ask what she liked to eat at dinner but he had, without the smallest hesitation, put himself in the path of what he thought might be a knife to protect her. Kat was stunned but hopelessly impressed that he could even have considered putting himself at risk for her benefit.

'Wouldn't your security have taken care of him?' she prompted in bewilderment.

'Their primary task is always to protect me, not those I am with. It was *my* duty to protect you, *milaya moya,*' Mikhail growled between compressed lips, a lean brown hand clenching into a fist on his thigh, his adrenalin charge still clearly running on a high.

'For what it's worth, thanks.' Kat concentrated on breathing in deep and slow to still her racing heartbeat.

'You were in no danger—it was only a camera,' Mikhail reminded her dismissively.

But *he* hadn't known that when he had instinctively acted to ensure that she was not hurt, Kat conceded, suddenly plunged deep into her own thoughts and ashamed of the speed with which she had been willing to label Mikhail as selfish and arrogant. What had just happened revealed that there was far more depth and many more shades to the Russian billionaire's tough character than she had been prepared to believe.

When Mikhail stepped into the lift with her back at the hotel, however, Kat's nervous tension mushroomed afresh. She wondered why he was coming up to the suite with her. He lounged back in one corner of the lift, brilliant black eyes pinned to her with glittering intensity, and her legs went all woolly and her head swam, nerves fluttering in her tummy as she fumbled for something casual to say to dispel the dangerous drag in the atmosphere.

'What birth sign are you?' Kat heard herself ask inanely.

Mikhail gazed back at her blankly. No, she wasn't going to get any horoscope chit-chat out of him, she registered in fierce embarrassment.

'I'm a Leo...I was asking when were you born?' Kat explained in the hope that he would appreciate that she wasn't a crackpot.

Mikhail, taken aback by the random nature of the conversation and still not grasping what she wanted from him, breathed tentatively, 'Thirty years ago?'

In receipt of that unexpected information, Kat froze in horror. 'Are you telling me that you're only thirty years old?' She gasped.

Exasperated, Mikhail, who had been thinking that kissing her would hardly be breaking the rules because it was essential that she became accustomed to being touched by him, raised level black brows in enquiry. '*Ya ne poni' mayu*...I don't understand. What's the problem? What are we talking about?'

Kat's back was so stiff she might have had a poker welded to her slender spine and her colour remained high. She stepped out of the lift, dipped the key card into the lock on the suite door and stalked into the big reception room, switching on the lights.

Mikhail followed her, a frown hardening his features as he studied her. 'Kat?' he pressed impatiently.

Kat spun back to him and settled furious green eyes on him. 'You're younger than me...*years* younger!' she launched at him in angry consternation. 'I can't believe that I didn't see that, that I didn't even consider the possibility!'

Unmoved by the same conflict of emotion that powered Kat, Mikhail gazed steadily back at her. '*Da*... you're a few years older. And the problem *is*?'

Outrage shimmering through her slender taut figure, Kat stared back at him accusingly. '*That's* a big problem as far as I'm concerned.'

Women were strange, Mikhail reflected, but he was utterly convinced in that instant that she was more strange than most. She had been born five years in advance of him. It was an age difference so minor in his opinion that it was barely worth commenting on, but the look of aversion stamped in her beautiful green eyes warned him that she was not so accepting of the fact. Anger stirred in him because he immediately recognised that she was grabbing at yet another reason to hold him at bay and no woman had ever put up such sustained resistance to him before.

'It's not a problem for me,' Mikhail countered curtly, black eyes brooding as he struggled to work out why he still wanted her in spite of all the discouragement she offered. In fact the more she tried to move away, the faster he wanted to haul her back in a kneejerk reaction that felt natural enough to disturb him.

An older woman with a younger man, Kat was thinking in painful mortification. People always found that combination both funny and objectionable. Remarkably older men seemed to get away with relationships with very young women without attracting similar derision. But the knowledge that Mikhail was a full five years younger than she was simply underscored Kat's conviction that she should not be with him at all.

'It's wrong, distasteful…inappropriate that you're younger than I am,' Kat spelt out jerkily. 'I've read in the newspapers about women christened "cougars" for getting involved with younger men and I'm afraid I've never wanted a toy boy…'

A smouldering silence spread between them.

'A toy boy? You are calling *me* a toy boy?' Mikhail echoed in rampant disbelief that she could have *dared* to apply that offensive term to him. Dark blood marked the arch of his high cheekbones. It was one of the very few occasions in his life when he was rendered almost mute by a shock backed by a surge of the volatile rage that he virtually never let anyone see. 'Take that back… that term,' he instructed rawly. 'It is an insult that no man would tolerate!'

The scorching heat of his dark eyes blazing with indignation clashed with Kat's defiant gaze. She was very still because although he had not raised his voice she had never seen that much anger in anyone: it burned off him like a shower of sparks in darkness, acting on her like a menacing wave of warning that shortened the breath in her lungs and convulsed her throat.

'You're years younger than me,' Kat responded in shaken self-defence, pained by that discovery, not even understanding why it should matter so much to her. 'It's not right—'

'Take it back,' Mikhail breathed wrathfully. 'It is unacceptable that you should say such a thing to me.'

Kat swallowed hard. Her knees felt wobbly: he really could be the most downright intimidating male. 'All right, I'll take it back,' she muttered ruefully. 'I didn't intend to insult you but I was shocked.'

'I would be no woman's toy boy,' Mikhail delivered harshly.

It was a ludicrous label for a six-foot-five-inch male exuding aggression, Kat conceded numbly as she sank down boneless with stress on a sofa and nodded weakly, still shaken by the inexplicable emotions that had erupted inside her. 'Well, that's OK because I wouldn't make a very good cougar,' she confided in a pained undertone.

'Why not?' Mikhail enquired, his tension dispersing as he studied her. She looked exhausted, her russet head drooping on her slender neck like a broken flower, as if it was too much effort to hold it upright, and a sense of blame assailed him because he had almost lost his temper with her and he knew he had frightened her. He recalled his father's infamous violent rages too well to allow himself any comparable outlet. Indeed the main bastion of his character was self-control in every mood and in every situation.

Kat was all shaken up. She could not recall ever having been in such turmoil before or understanding herself less. He was only thirty-years old and she was thirty five, way too old for him, in fact even being attracted to him was practically cradle-snatching, she decided desolately.

'Why not?' Mikhail asked again, curious about what

made her tick in a way he had never been curious about a woman before.

'Cougars are experienced women…I'm not,' Kat admitted dully, convinced that she was an oddity in such a day and age and wondering in despair how she could possibly have done things differently. Her mother had put her sisters through so much with her ever-changing parade of men and Kat knew that for the sake of her siblings' welfare she needed to lead a very different life from Odette. Unfortunately ten years earlier she had not appreciated that that would mean celibacy because in those days she had still dimly assumed that eventually she would meet a suitable man and enjoy a serious relationship. Only it hadn't happened; the opportunity had just never arisen.

His level black brows drew together. 'I don't understand.'

Kat released a bitter laugh that was discordant in the quiet room and lifted scornful green eyes to say, 'I'm still a virgin. How's that for seriously weird?'

In the immediate aftermath of that admission, it would have been hard to say which of them was the more shocked: Kat that she had told him something she had never told any other living person, or Mikhail, who could not have been more stunned had she confessed that she was a serial killer. Physical innocence was way beyond his experience and even further removed from his comfort level.

CHAPTER SIX

ENSCONCED IN THE spectacular luxury of Mikhail's private jet the following day on a flight to Cyprus where they were to board his yacht, *The Hawk,* Kat pretended to read a magazine.

So far, Mikhail had not required much in the way of companionship. He had worked industriously since they boarded mid-morning. If he wasn't talking on his phone, he was doing something on his laptop or rapping out instructions to the employee who had boarded with him. Kat was relieved by his detachment because she was still cringing over her behaviour with him the night before. How on earth had she lost the plot like that? Why the heck had she randomly announced that she was a virgin? That was none of his business and totally extraneous information to a male she had no plans to become intimate with. She would live to be a hundred before she forgot the stunned expression he had worn in receipt of her gauche admission. Aghast at having embarrassed herself to that extent, Kat had simply fled afterwards, muttering goodnight and taking refuge in her bedroom.

A *virgin*? Mikhail was still brooding on that astounding information. It explained a lot about her though, he conceded grudgingly; it made sense of things he hadn't understood. No wonder she had been so edgy and had overreacted to his approach in her home, no wonder she had felt the need to insist that she would not sleep with him! But he was still strongly disconcerted that a beautiful, sensual woman with so vital a spirit could have denied herself physical pleasure for so many years. His suspicion that she might be trying to play games with him as so many of her predecessors had done by using his desire for her as a bargaining chip had died then and there. Furthermore, far from being daunted by what she had told him, he had discovered that he wanted her more than ever. Was that because she had never been with another man? The novelty of the situation? It was yet another question he couldn't answer. He studied her covertly, taking in the taut delicacy of her profile set against her rich russet curls and the long slender legs crossed at the knee with a humming tension he could feel. Although he knew that she wasn't one bit happy about being on his jet en route to his yacht, hunger laced with satisfaction roared through Mikhail like a tornado. For the moment, she was here and she was *his*. Pushing his laptop aside, he dismissed the PA hovering at his elbow to do his bidding.

Kat stole a covert glance at Mikhail, yielding to the terrible secret fascination that literally consumed her in his presence and tugged at her every nerve-ending. She sensed his preoccupation, wondered if he was thinking about her and despised herself for it. She didn't want his attention, had never wanted his interest, she told herself staunchly. Yet how did that belief tie in with her treacherous satisfaction that he should find her so attractive? There was something within her that rejoiced in his awareness and her own, something she didn't know how to root out, something that scared her because it seemed outside her control.

'Would you like a drink?' Mikhail asked smoothly.

'Water, just water, please…' Kat responded, mouth running dry as she collided with glittering black eyes enhanced by luxuriant lashes. Alcohol would not be a good idea when she needed to keep her wits about her. He had the most *stunning* eyes and the reflection made colour stream like a banner across her cheekbones.

Mikhail pressed the bell and the steward appeared to serve them. Restive as a prowling jungle cat, Mikhail leapt upright and watched her sip almost frantically at the water, the glass in her slender hand trembling almost infinitesimally. She could fight it all she liked, he thought with dark triumph, but she was every bit as aware of him as he was of her. He reached down, deftly removing the glass from her clinging fingers to set it aside, closing a big hand over hers to lift her to her feet. She raised startled eyes to his lean strong face, her beautiful eyes as verdant a green as a spring leaf.

'*What*?' Kat gasped, nerves now leaping about like jumping beans inside her as she looked up at him, feeling dwarfed by his height and width, the sheer hard power of his tall, well-built frame.

'I'm going to kiss you,' Mikhail murmured huskily, his dark deep drawl roughening.

Totally unprepared for that approach, her lashes flickered in shock. '*But*—'

'I don't need permission for a kiss,' Mikhail derided. 'Only to take you to bed. That gives me a fair amount of leeway, *milaya moya*.'

Kat was very much shaken by that catastrophic interpretation of their agreement. She had assumed that if he could accept she wouldn't sleep with him, he wouldn't touch her at all, for why would he want to waste time and energy on foreplay when the main event was not on offer to close the deal? She was stung by the realisation that he was bending the rules and by the belief that she should have known in her bones how devious he would be.

'But I don't want this,' Kat told him feverishly, her slender body rigid as steel in the imprisoning circle of his arms.

'Let me show you what you want,' Mikhail husked with unassailable cool, long fingers closing into a handful of russet curls to draw her head back.

And he kissed her with soul-shattering intensity, his lips hungrily demanding entrance to her mouth, his tongue tangling erotically with hers and stabbing deep enough to send streamers of liquid fire snaking through her trembling body. She had had kisses, but nothing had ever come close to comparing to that explosive assault. That kiss was utterly decadent and deeply, compellingly sexual in nature. Suddenly her bra felt too small and tight to contain her swelling breasts. Her nipples were almost painfully stiff and the tingling awareness there tugged as though a piece of elastic connected her breasts to her groin. The tender flesh between her legs felt hot and damp and unbearably sensitive.

A big hand splayed across her bottom, gathering her closer, so that her breasts were crushed by the wall of his chest and she could feel the bold, hard ridge of his erection against her. A dulled ache gripped her pelvis, heat pulsing at her feminine core, and her knees turned weak and boneless beneath her.

His black hair tousled by her fingers, Mikhail lifted his dark head to stare down at the hectically flushed triangle of her face. 'You see...' he murmured raggedly, reining back his overwhelming need with fierce self-discipline, determined not to destroy the moment. 'There's nothing to be scared of.'

Breathless, Kat reeled away from him again, shattered by the effect he had had on her and the mindless clamour of a body suddenly unplugged from the source of energy and excitement that he had taught her to crave. Nothing to be scared of? Was he joking? Every natural alarm she possessed was screaming panic at full volume. Purebred predator that he was, he was toying with her as a cat might play with a mouse, his confidence in his own powers of seduction supreme. And why shouldn't he feel like that? Kat castigated herself furiously. Telling a guy like Mikhail that she was a virgin had been the equivalent of throwing down a red carpet to welcome the enemy.

Let me show you what you want. How dared he? As if she didn't know what she wanted; as if she were so confused it would take a *man* to show her anything! She already knew that he attracted her but she wasn't prepared to act on the fact. Her choice, her decision! Trembling with rage and frustration, she sank back into her seat and refused to look at him again. He would use her own weakness against her without conscience but she was stronger than that, much stronger. Her teeth clenched together hard as she bit back angry defensive words that would only tell him how rattled she was. He had done that to her. With one scorching kiss he had pulled the rug out from below her feet.

Mikhail savoured his vodka, blithely unconcerned by the furious silence emanating from his companion. So, she was angry, but he had expected that: she was a fiery, independent woman too accustomed to having her own way. He wasn't going to back off like a little boy who had had his wrist slapped and it was better that she knew the score from the outset. He had trod on glass around her for long enough. That wasn't his style with a woman and now it was time for him to be himself.

When the jet landed in Cyprus, they transferred to a helicopter. The noise of the rotor blades on board made conversation impossible. As the unwieldy craft came in to land on the pad on the prow of the huge yacht below them, Kat was wide-eyed with wonderment. *The Hawk* was much bigger than she had expected and infinitely more elegant, different decks rising in sleek tiers rimmed with gleaming metal balustrades. There was already another pair of helicopters parked nearby.

'I wasn't expecting anything this size,' Kat confessed as Mikhail urged her away from the landing area with a predictably bossy hand planted to her spine.

A grin slashed his wide mobile mouth and he told her what length *The Hawk* was and the maximum speed it travelled at. His zeal and pride of possession were patent and Kat listened graciously to the story of where the yacht was built, who he had chosen to design it and why as well as the exact specifications he offered. Although Kat had very little interest in such matters and much of it was too technical for her, she did have a fond memory of her late father giving her equally enthusiastic and unnecessary details about a new lawnmower he had once bought. The comparison almost made her laugh, for she knew that Mikhail would hang, draw and quarter her if he knew she had likened his precious yacht to a piece of garden machinery.

After a man in a captain's cap greeted Mikhail and a brief introduction was performed, Kat moved away a few feet to stand by the guard rail, the breeze blowing her hair back from her face as she took in the impressive view of the sleek prow scything smoothly through the turquoise depths of the Mediterranean sea. It was an undeniably beautiful day: the sky was blue and the sun was shining down to pour welcome warmth on her winter-chilled skin and, annoyed as she still was with Mikhail, she could only feel glad to be alive on such a day.

A stewardess in uniform appeared at her elbow, told Kat that her name was Marta and offered to show her to her cabin. Leaving Mikhail chatting to the captain, Kat followed the stewardess down an incredible curving glass staircase, which Marta informed her lit up and changed colours once darkness fell. Quite why anyone would want a staircase that changed colour escaped Kat, but the sheer opulence of the guest suite impressed her to death. The bed in the big room sat on a shallow dais and doors led off to an incredible marble bathroom, a dressing room and a private furnished balcony. A steward arrived with Kat's luggage and Marta proceeded to unpack it.

'When do the other guests arrive?' Kat enquired.

'In about an hour, Miss Marshall,' Marta told her.

Positively relieved by the news that she and Mikhail were not to be left alone together for even a day, Kat decided to get changed to ensure that she was ready for her hostessing duties. Choosing a simple but elegant toffee-coloured shift dress from her new wardrobe, she freshened up in the bathroom, emerging just as another door opened on the far side of her room and Mikhail strode in.

'You're dressed…excellent,' he pronounced approvingly.

Through the door he had left open behind him she could see another bedroom, which she surmised to be his and her colour heightened as dismay flashed through her. 'There's a connecting door between your accommodation and mine?'

A wickedly amused smile slashed his expressive mouth. He stood there, big and bold and brazen, daring her to object. 'Did you expect me to have it bricked up for your benefit?'

Her small white teeth scissored together. 'Of course not, but for future reference…I'll be keeping it locked—'

'I have a master key for every compartment on board but you don't need to be quite so protective of your privacy—I'm equally keen on my own,' Mikhail informed her drily while simultaneously awarding her slender figure a slow, lingering appraisal that ran from the top of her head down to her curling toes. Beneath that relentless dark and shameless gaze, fresh heat sprang up in her face and her discomfiture increased. 'That colour suits you—I knew it would.'

Kat was already very tense. 'You chose my clothes… *personally*?'

'Why not? I've been buying clothes for my women since I was eighteen,' Mikhail fielded with lazy assurance.

It was just another piece of his control freakery, Kat told herself in exasperation, not something she needed to get worked up about. Unfortunately there was something alarmingly intimate about the idea that he had personally selected the very clothes she wore to suit his tastes. That was way too intimate. She had assumed some hired help had selected the garments. And she really didn't want to know that he had been buying clothes for women since he was a teenager. That both shocked and alienated her. The very thought of him with other women was offensive to her and the discovery filled her with consternation. Surely she couldn't be developing possessive feelings about him?

'I'm not *your* woman,' Kat told him with icy emphasis, green eyes glimmering with hauteur and resentment.

'Then what are you?' Mikhail countered levelly, one ebony brow slightly elevated as if he was looking forward to the prospect of her trying to explain her exact role in his life.

'Your hostess…er, your companion,' Kat quantified stiltedly.

A charismatic smile of amusement crossed his face. His spectacular eyes glittered like black diamonds in sunshine, his potent sexual appeal making her mouth run dry and her blood run hot in a way she was starting to recognise. With great difficulty she dragged her gaze from his, struggling to control the race of her heartbeat and the edge-of-her-seat excitement he could induce so easily.

'I'm not *your* woman,' Kat told him stubbornly again.

'But never doubt that that's my ultimate goal, *milaya moya,*' Mikhail imparted silkily just as a knock sounded on the door.

It was the dynamic blonde, Lara, from his London office. Her bright blue eyes ping-ponged assessingly between her employer and Kat before she extended a file to Mikhail, which he immediately passed to Kat. 'The profiles of the guests I've invited,' he explained.

Kat's fingers tightened round the file while she told herself that Mikhail's goal was not a threat to her as long as she kept a steady head on her shoulders. This holiday on his yacht was an interlude in her life, not a real part of it. 'Thanks. I'll study them.'

And with a decisive jerk of his chin, Mikhail swung

round and returned to his own room. Kat followed him
at speed and snapped shut the lock on the door before
walking out to the balcony and sitting down on a comfortable wicker seat to open the file.

There were twenty guests in all, more than she had
expected. There were several business tycoons with
their partners and adult children as well as a well-
known entrepreneur and his actress girlfriend. Some
of the names were familiar to her, most were not. The
presentation of the file, however, had calmed her nerves
because it was a welcome reminder that she was on *The
Hawk* to fulfil a function and she intended to do it to
the best of her ability as she memorised the useful information she had been given.

An hour later, Lara reappeared to usher her upstairs
to welcome Mikhail's guests, who had arrived on the
helicopters sent to collect them. Lara had changed into
a very short silver dress more akin to a cocktail frock
than anything else and it had the effect of making Kat
feel severely underdressed. She reminded herself that
Mikhail had approved what she wore but that was a
humbling recollection that could only irritate her. After
all, she was not *his* woman; she did not belong to him
in any way and she had no intention of changing her
mind on that score.

The salon was a large light-filled space ornamented
with spectacular seating arrangements and paintings.
Lara hovering at her elbow, Kat spoke to a well-pre-
served blonde in a reassuringly restrained dress. Even
so, a glance around the gathered cliques revealed the
fact that all the younger guests were wearing party gear,
displaying legs, cleavage and glitzy jewellery. A slight
hush fell in the chatter and the hair at the nape of Kat's
neck prickled a sixth-sense warning. She turned her

head to see Mikhail stride in, dressed in tailored chino trousers and an open shirt. The sheer impact of his size, black hair and golden skin was undeniable and set up a sizzling chain reaction deep in her ~~~~~~~ sketching her shift her feet uncomfortably. She saw the women present look at him as though he were a tasty dish on a banqueting table and move almost as one towards him until he was literally surrounded.

'Women always act that way around the boss. You'll get used to it,' Lara cooed in her ear in a saccharine-sweet tone of sympathy.

'It doesn't bother me,' Kat fielded softly, pride making her chin tilt, and stiffening her spine. Mikhail was breathtakingly handsome and sexy in a way she had never seen in a man before but she could cope, yes, she could cope because looks and sex appeal were only a superficial blessing. She had no intention of getting involved in a shallow affair with a man who was only interested in her body.

Lara gave her an unconvinced look and said, 'Most women are prepared to put up with a lot to stay in the boss's life.'

'I'm quite content,' Kat responded evasively, uneasy with the conversation and how personal it was becoming because she wasn't sure whether or not any of Mikhail's staff were aware that she was simply a woman hired to do a job and she did not want to be indiscreet. After all, Birkside hung in the balance and, while Mikhail's ultimate goal seemed to be sexual, Kat's sole goal was to reclaim her home. And she *would* achieve that, she told herself bracingly, without sex playing any part in the arrangement.

'That's Lorne Arnold over there,' Lara whispered, evidently having taken the hint that her curiosity was unwelcome. 'I would pay him some special attention. He looks bored.'

Kat nodded, her brain summoning up the details she ~~ally memorised.~~ Lorne Arnold. At thirty-three years of age, he was a very successful London-based property developer and he was currently involved in a high-profile development scheme with Mikhail. He was an attractive man with blond hair almost long enough to hit his shoulders and his partner, Mel, a top financial analyst, was nowhere to be seen. Possibly the woman had decided to change before she joined them, Kat surmised, directing her steps into his path while she moved a hand towards a waiter standing by the wall to encourage him to bring his tray of drinks over.

Mikhail's brooding gaze swept the room and snapped to a sudden halt when he finally located his target. His big powerful frame went rigid. Kat was laughing and smiling up at Lorne Arnold. He watched in growing disbelief as Lorne planted a hand to Kat's arm to draw her attention to a painting on the wall and guided her over to it, and his handsome mouth compressed into a harsh line, rage lashing through him like a whip. What the hell did Lorne think he was playing at when he flirted with Kat of all people? And why was Kat encouraging him like that? That was certainly not the way she behaved in Mikhail's company when she had never yet deigned to laugh or smile. Kat still treated Mikhail like a queen trying to repel an over-familiar commoner and it galled him. The only time he was happy with her response to him was when she was in his arms and her reserve was shattered, ripped away by the passion she could not suppress.

'*Ty v poryadka*...are you OK?' Stas murmured to one side of him.

Eyes bright as golden stars in his lean strong face, Mikhail was pale with dark fury and he didn't trust himself to speak. Kat was engaged in animated conversation with Lorne: her expressive hands were cl~~~~ vivid word pictures while she studied the painting with the other man. Lorne now had an arm clasped round her waist and the sight of that familiarity was so offensive to Mikhail that he could happily have wrenched the couple apart and tossed his business partner off the side of the yacht. Kat was *his*. She's *mine* screamed every fibre of Mikhail's tautly muscled body and he was ready to break Lorne's arms for daring to touch her. Damn art, Mikhail thought bitterly, thrusting his passage through the crush around him. That had to be the common denominator that had brought down the barriers between Kat and Lorne because Lorne was involved with the Arts Council and *she* had a degree in Fine Arts. Mikhail's vast and much-admired art collection was solely investment-based and he couldn't have talked about any of it, for his interest had never gone much beyond that level. And for the first time in his life he was in no mood to admit to being a total philistine.

An arm locked round Kat's waist from behind, anchoring her back into the powerful strength and heat of a large male body. Disconcerted at being touched without warning even though she knew immediately who it was who held her, Kat jerked and froze even as Mikhail murmured her name above her head and addressed Lorne Arnold. Hot pink swept her cheeks as the other man tensed, unable to hide his surprise at Mikhail's revealing embrace. Long lean fingers brushed her torrent of russet curls back off one slim shoulder and male lips slowly grazed the slender column of her throat, pressing in at one point in a fleeting kiss that sent a lightning bolt of sizzling sexual awareness shooting through her unprepared body. Her breasts peaked and sliding heat clenched every muscle in her pelvis. Even as angry resentment roared through Kat she found herself leaning back into Mikhail for support to compensate for the sudden paralysing weakness of her legs.

'Excuse us,' Mikhail purred like the predator he was, holding Kat below one arm like a piece of booty he had reclaimed and urging her across the room while at the same time refusing to allow any of his attentive guests to intercept him.

Stas yanked open the door in readiness and Kat recognised the glimmer of amusement in the older man's eyes even though his expression was politely impassive. That glimpse stoked her own temper even more and that was the only reason she did not protest Mikhail's domineering behaviour. She did not want to have a row with Mikhail in front of an interested audience.

Thrust into another room across the corridor furnished like an office, Kat barely paused to draw breath before she whirled round to confront him. 'How dare you touch me like that in public?' she raked at him in an uncompromising attack.

Mikhail was utterly taken aback by that defiant demand, and his darkly handsome features hardened even more. 'You shouldn't have been flirting with him and encouraging him to take liberties—'

'I wasn't flirting with him!' Kat flung back at him hotly. 'We were just chatting—'

'*Nyet*…no, you were flirting like mad, batting your eyelashes…smiling…*giggling*!' Mikhail condemned in a raw undertone of accusation, eyes full of derision at her plea of innocence.

Belatedly recognising that he was entirely serious

in his misapprehension, Kat compressed her lips. 'We were in a room surrounded by people—'

'And I saw in his face that until I touched you he didn't even realise who you were!' Mikhail grated. 'He would never have laid a finger on you had he known you were here with me. You should have been by my side—'

Kat tilted her bright head to one side, green eyes sharp as lasers with offence. 'Sticking to you like glue, so that you didn't feel the need to mark your territory like a wolf? I have never been so embarrassed in my life.'

Black eyes blazing at her accusation, Mikhail bit out ferociously, 'Don't exaggerate! I only kissed your neck—I didn't touch you anywhere intimate!'

Still all too aware of the fast-beating pulse at the precise spot he had *only* kissed, Kat went rigid with resentment at the memory of the practised manner in which he had demolished any possible resistance she might have raised to protect herself. That place on her throat was clearly an erogenous zone she had not even known she possessed and he was a man capable of demonstrating many more such tricks. Well, he wouldn't be doing that to her again—not if she had anything to do with it!

'I wasn't flirting,' she said again in a cutting tone and she watched him pick up on that tone as if she had thrown a flaming torch at him: his black eyes suddenly burning jewel-bright, his exotic cheekbones slashing taut. 'Why would I have flirted with him? Lorne has a girlfriend and I was expecting her to appear at any moment—'

'When he arrived, he told me they'd broken up a few weeks ago. He's looking for a replacement and he had his eye on you,' Mikhail delivered grimly.

Refusing to be intimidated, Kat tossed her russet

curls back and sighed. 'So? I smiled at the man. I was only being friendly. I don't giggle…I never ever giggle,' she told him drily. 'And you didn't like it? Why do you think that is? Because I don't smile and laugh with you? Ask yourself if you have ever done or said *anything* likely to encourage such a relaxed response from me.'

Infuriated by the charge that laid fault at his door when it was her unacceptable behaviour that had provoked him into warning off Lorne, Mikhail gritted his perfect white teeth and almost snarled. He reached out for her with determined hands.

Kat backed off so fast that she would have fallen over, had she not had the support of the desk behind her. 'You're such a caveman,' she muttered helplessly. 'And you're not touching me in that mood.'

Mikhail stayed where he was mere inches from her but he dropped his hands, disconcerted by her words and equally disturbed by the level of his own anger. 'I would never ever hurt you.'

And reading the look of reproach in his stunning eyes, Kat believed him, but he was never going to be a pussycat of the domestic variety either. He was one-hundred-per-cent primal male laced with aggression. 'I know but unfortunately for both of us that legal agreement didn't go far enough—'

'Kat…?' Mikhail began darkly, exasperated by the change of subject.

'No, please let me have my say for once,' Kat cut in in a resolute plea that ignored the taut silence smouldering around her. 'You want something from me that I'm not prepared to give and now you're judging me unfairly. I wouldn't flirt with one of your guests. I'm not that sort of woman, I'm not even sure that after so long I even know how to flirt any more—'

'You *know*,' Mikhail contradicted without hesitation. 'Lorne couldn't take his eyes off you.'

'But I was only trying to make him feel welcome. There was no subtext and nothing else intended,' Kat told him quietly. 'I wouldn't do anything to embarrass you either but you *do* need to be aware of the boundaries of that agreement.'

'In what way?' Mikhail prompted, marvelling that against all odds she had managed to talk him down from his rage, somehow cutting through all the aggro to make him think clearly again. Even so, he didn't like the explosive, unpredictable effect she had on his mood; he didn't like it at all. Lorne was a business partner and a friend, but, if the other man had gone even one step further with Kat, Mikhail knew he would have struck him. The sight of Lorne's hand on Kat had enraged him and that disturbed him as well. In all fairness, what could have happened between Lorne and Kat in a room full of people? Nothing, his logic answered. He had never been a possessive man when it came to women but Kat roused unsettling reactions in him. He didn't want another man anywhere near her. But where did she get off calling him a caveman? He was a highly sophisticated, educated guy, who had never treated a woman in a less than civilised manner. Had he been the barbarian she suggested he would already have seduced her and dragged her off to his bed, instead of which he was, for the first time in his life, practising restraint with a woman and giving her the chance to get to know him... for all the good that that was doing him, he reflected broodingly as he recalled the caveman insult.

Mikhail shifted an infinitesimal distance closer and her big green eyes widened. Beautiful eyes but not doe's eyes. Kat's eyes were wide, wary, and suspicious. He lifted a hand and ran his forefinger gently down the side of her face. 'In what way do I need to be aware?'

Kat blinked. For a split second her entire mind was a terrifying, disorientating blank. The touch of his finger had whispered down her cheekbone like a teasing caress and he was so close her nostrils were flaring on the spicy tang of the cologne he wore and the underlying scent of clean warm male. Butterflies broke loose in her tummy, her nipples tightening and lengthening below her clothing. 'Aware?' she queried uncertainly.

'You said I had to be aware of the boundaries of our legal agreement,' Mikhail reminded her, black-lashed dark eyes turned a mesmeric gold as they connected with hers.

Like a doll re-equipped with a new battery, Kat's brain suddenly switched back on. 'Oh, yes, the agreement. I think you need to be reminded that you don't own me. I don't belong to you in any way—'

'Nor do you belong to anyone else,' Mikhail pointed out with lethal cool. 'You're up for grabs—'

'No, I'm not!' Kat countered speedily, keen to kick that idea to the kerb. 'I'm not interested in a relationship with anyone—'

'Except with me,' Mikhail slotted in silkily, as stubborn as a mule in pursuit of his goal.

Oh, my word, those long curling eyelashes went for her every time he got close, a quite unnecessary dramatic embellishment to his stunning dark gaze, Kat reflected dizzily. Her mouth was running dry, her brain on overload, physical impressions flooding her and washing away logical thought.

'You want me,' Mikhail told her with a deep roughened edge to his powerful voice that shimmied down her taut spine and made her tremble.

Without any warning that she picked up on, he framed her face with long splayed fingers and kissed her. It was drugging, wildly intoxicating, like an adrenalin shot straight into the veins. One minute she was thinking no, this *can't* happen, I must stop it here and now, and the next the hungry and continuing pressure of that wide sensual mouth was what she wanted and needed most in the world.

With a muffled sound thrumming deep in his broad chest, Mikhail gathered her up into his arms and sank down in the chair behind the desk. For a split second he appraised her flushed and lovely face, the dazed expression in her eyes for once empty of defiance and censure, and it grabbed hold of every base male instinct in his body. He wanted her so much more than he had ever wanted any other woman. He wanted her under him, over him, in every possible position. He wanted her to accept that she was *his*. He wanted to see that look of bliss on her face for him again and again and again. Tamping down his ferocious hunger to possess, he lifted her up to him and darted his tongue between her lips in a rhythmic invasion, revelling in the sweetness of her response and the little moan she could not hold back.

'*Ti takaya krasivaya*…you are so beautiful…' he translated his own first words for her '…but *ti svodishme nya suma*…' You drive me crazy.' He didn't translate that last admission.

As he bent over her Kat's fingertips feathered through his thick black hair even while she was wondering what she was doing, but, strangely enough, she felt extraordinarily safe and at peace in his arms. There was something definitely to be said for a male big enough and strong enough to pick her up. 'What am I doing?' she framed with a sudden frown.

'For once? Exactly what you want,' Mikhail husked and kissed her again with all the hungry fervour of his high-voltage temperament.

With one hand he nudged her knees apart and she tensed, a choky little sound of dismay escaping her throat.

'I won't do anything you don't want me to do. I won't take you.' Mikhail was determined to keep her where she was on his lap and within reach of intimacies he had hitherto only been able to dream about.

The tension in her slender frame began to ebb and he nibbled enticingly at her full lower lip before plunging his tongue deep within again. The taste of him went to her head like fine wine and another flush of arousal travelled through her, stiffening her nipples and making her achingly aware of an even more private place. He pushed up the hem of her skirt and she jerked while he made soothing sounds she could not have believed he was capable of making. His hand smoothed over her inner thigh, temptingly close to the unbearable heat and sensitivity there, and she had never wanted so badly in her life to be touched. The need for more was screaming through her every skin cell like nothing she had ever imagined and so strong was that need she consciously stopped trying to fight it. Curiosity had awakened along with the longing.

He stroked a finger over the stretched taut fabric of her knickers, heat rippled through her and her hips rose and her slender thighs parted without her volition. 'Just do it…w-whatever,' she murmured shakily from between clenched teeth for she truly didn't know what he was planning to do and didn't much care at that moment. If he could satisfy the desperate pulsing craving inside her, it would be enough.

Mikhail almost laughed at that command she had issued but the strangest shard of something tender burnished his hard dark eyes. He didn't know what it was about her but she touched things in him that nobody else ever had and right then she needed him. He closed his lips to her wonderfully swollen and tempting mouth and wrenched the surprisingly strong barrier of her underwear down her legs, even sparing a frowning glance in the item's direction as it fell on the floor in a sensible heap of white cotton, for it was certainly not anything that had featured in his lingerie choices for her wardrobe.

One moment Kat was mortifyingly aware of how damp she was down below and the next as a fingertip very delicately traced the tiny entrance to her body she was shivering and mindless with a flood of hunger like nothing she had ever felt before. There was not a thought in her head—there was no room for it: excitement had driven out everything else. He stroked her clitoris and it was as if an electric shock ran through her, her back arching, every muscle tightening. He circled that tiny bundle of nerve-endings and it was like being set on fire, for the tormented shivers of arousal were assailing her ever more strongly. The heat in her pelvis and the extreme sensitivity at the heart of her were almost unbearable. His tongue flicked against the roof of her mouth and she gasped round it as he eased a finger into her, answering a need she had not even known she had until he showed her. She bucked. Erotic pulses of agonisingly strong sensation were gathering at her feminine core and she couldn't stay still, couldn't find her voice to tell him that she needed *more* and *faster*. And almost as though he was attuned to her needs as she was, his fingers plunged deeper within her while his thumb pressed against her clitoris.

'Come for me, *laskovaya moya*,' Mikhail husked, a tremor she had never heard before threading his voice.

And there was nothing Kat chose about what happened next, for her body had long since taken charge of her. It was as if white lightning cracked inside her, throwing her high and tearing her apart while wave after wave of shudderingly intense pleasure engulfed her.

But Kat didn't float back to planet earth again, she fell with a resounding crash when coherent thought returned and she grasped exactly what she had allowed. And she wanted to scream and thump herself, was already wondering if she was a split personality to tell him to stay away, to tell herself that she wanted him to stay away and then to engage in such intimacy!

'I want so much more from you,' Mikhail confessed huskily, both arms banded round her so firmly that she would've had to fight to escape.

Kat couldn't look at him, knew the power of those eyes of his to sway her into stupidity and recklessness. 'Please let go of me,' she whispered unevenly, desperate to find the right words to explain herself but meeting only a mortifying emptiness in her brain. Confusion assailed her. Only the awareness that it had been a very one-sided episode restrained the anger she usually used to keep him at a safer distance.

Mikhail expelled his breath in a thwarted hiss and released her with exaggerated immediacy. Dragging the hem of her dress down over her thighs, Kat scooped up the undergarment on the floor with crimson cheeks. 'I don't know what to say to you—'

'Say nothing at all,' Mikhail advised in a dry tone

that made her wince. 'You're not very tactful. Go and change for dinner. I'll see you later.'

Later…as in her bedroom? Kat wondered wildly. Well, she could hardly blame the guy for expecting something in return for such encouragement as she had given him! Nor could she imagine managing to tell him that lust wasn't enough, for her, would never be enough for that, she was convinced, was what was wrong with her. She lusted after him like a shameless hussy, lost all control the minute he looked at her in a certain way or made physical contact!

Mikhail swore long and low in Russian. She was nuts, way too mixed-up for him. How had he avoided seeing that for so long? What *was* he doing with her? He should have her flown home, allow Lara to take over… That would be the rational thing to do. And Mikhail was nothing if he was not rational.

CHAPTER SEVEN

FIVE DAYS LATER, Mikhail stood on the terrace outside his office on *The Hawk* sharing a drink with Lorne Arnold.

His other guests were swimming and sunbathing down below on the main deck. He was so accustomed to half-naked women that he spared the exposed bodies barely a glance, awarding his attention only to a slender redhead moving in the shadows. As willowy and graceful in her leggy delicacy as a gazelle, Kat burned in the sun, but her smooth light skin made her stand out all the more from his fake-tanned and sun-bronzed guests.

'Kat's a real find,' Lorne remarked carefully, watching Kat sit down with a book to read.

Mikhail gritted his even white teeth. If only you knew, he thought in frustration. He had backed off from Kat and that hadn't worked either. She was like a jigsaw puzzle with several missing pieces: incomprehensible and infuriating.

'Very natural, warm, unspoiled…' Lorne could not hide his appreciation

'Very unspoiled,' Mikhail fielded tongue-in-cheek.

'You don't seem to pay her much attention…'

'Kat thrives on neglect,' Mikhail told him grittily, wondering why he had had the misfortune to land the only woman in the world who didn't react to such an approach. Mikhail, more used to women who crowded him and clung, eager to please and entertain him, was at a rare loss with one who chose to keep her distance.

Lara settled down beside Kat in the shade. 'I'm too hot,' the svelte blonde complained.

Kat knew better than to suggest that the topless blonde in her minuscule bikini briefs take a dip in the inviting pool. Most of the female guests, including Lara, avoided the water to conserve their hair styling and make-up while Kat continued to swim several times a day, frustrated by the laziness of sitting around doing very little. It had made her hair a little frizzy but with a fully staffed beauty salon on board that was hardly a problem.

'Tonight is the guests' last night,' Lara reminded her. 'What are you wearing to the club in Ayia Napa?'

'I'll find something,' Kat responded lightly, watching Mikhail stand with a drink on his office terrace with Lorne. Very tall, very dark and very handsome and infuriatingly inscrutable and unpredictable. He had virtually ignored her since that fatal encounter in his office. While he was polite and gracious in company just as though they were a couple, he had not tried to touch her again and she didn't blame him for that, having looked back repeatedly to what she had done and cringed. She had *said* one thing to him but had *done* another. If he had had enough of that, so had she. It was as if she were a split personality, one half recalling her turbulent childhood with her man-hungry mother and the other half recalling the strict moral limits she had tried to instil in her sisters while always setting her siblings a good example. Sex to scratch an uncomfortable itch of lust didn't figure anywhere between those parameters and she was not ashamed of resisting the urge and standing by her principles.

'I hope you don't mind but I thought you might want to borrow something and I left a dress on your bed,' Lara told her with a bright smile.

In recent days, Kat had learned to relax more with the other Englishwoman, who had made a real effort to offer her useful advice. Gradually it had dawned on Kat that Lara usually hosted Mikhail's guests and could have bitterly resented being supplanted by Kat. For that reason the other woman's sociability had proved a pleasant surprise, particularly when compared to Mikhail's cool detachment.

'But I'm sure I've got—' Kat began in disconcertion.

'You haven't got anything suitable to wear to a nightclub,' Lara assured her confidently. 'You'll want to fit in…for a change.'

'My clubbing days are behind me,' Kat commented quietly, ignoring that less than tactful comment on her style. 'I'm thirty-five, Lara.'

Lara's eyes widened in apparent disbelief. 'But that means you're older than him! I'm only twenty-six.'

And probably much more suitable, Kat reflected wearily, wondering why that should bother her. Lara was beautiful and bright and posing there topless and uninhibited, infinitely more likely to please Mikhail than Kat ever could. Behind her sunglasses Kat focused on Mikhail, sunlight gleaming off his carved cheekbones and stubborn jaw line, and her heart seemed to twist at the very idea of him with Lara…with *any* woman. It was because she was dreaming about him every night, embarrassingly erotic dreams that made her wake up perspiring in a tangle of bedding.

A few hours later, garbed in Lara's short red dress

and buffed and polished within an inch of her life by the beauty salon, Kat scanned her reflection and grimaced. In her own opinion she was showing too much flesh because the dress bared her back and a good deal of her legs, but what was her opinion worth? She was a fish out of water in Mikhail's exclusive world and she didn't want to go clubbing with the younger, livelier members of the party and stick out like a sore thumb... like an older woman got up in absurdly teenaged clothing? Mutton dressed as lamb? Kat cringed at the fear that she might look foolish in the dress. A tide of homesickness suddenly engulfed her, accompanied by distaste for the superficial existence she was leading where appearance and amusement appeared to be all that truly mattered. Right at this very minute, her youngest sister, Topsy, was home from boarding school and staying at the farmhouse with Emmie, and although Kat phoned her sisters most days it wasn't the same as seeing them in the flesh and catching up on the gossip. Three more weeks marooned on Mikhail's giant floating palace threatened like a prison sentence.

Kat sat beside Lara in the VIP chill-out room where several yards away at another table Mikhail appeared to be holding court like a reigning king. Surrounded by bottles of champagne and beautiful girls vying for his attention, he was in his element.

'Is it always like this for Mikhail?' Kat heard herself ask her blonde companion.

Lara made no pretence of not grasping the question. 'You must understand that even when he was a boy he was very much in demand. He excites women because very rich, handsome and still *young* men are rare. They all want to be the one he marries but he doesn't want to get married.'

'That doesn't surprise me,' Kat responded, sliding upright to go to the cloakroom, glancing back over her shoulder at Mikhail to note that two young women in very revealing outfits were performing some ridiculous form of suggestive belly dance for him and his companions. Their giggling display of their nubile bodies set her teeth on edge and made her feel about a hundred years too old for such nonsense. Mikhail's arrogant dark head lifted and turned as though he could sense her watching him. Dark eyes gleaming, he summoned her with a lean brown hand to join him…as if she were a waitress or a pet dog or something! Stiffening at that suspicion, Kat reddened and ignored the signal. Her earlier attack of homesickness and alienation returned with even greater force. She didn't want to be in Cyprus at an exclusive club for the rich and bored. She didn't want to go back to Mikhail's yacht either. She didn't belong in either place and she missed her sisters.

She had persuaded herself that regaining the ownership of her home was worth any sacrifice and only now was she finally questioning that conviction. Mikhail was upsetting her. She could never remember feeling more unhappy than she currently felt and her self-esteem had sunk to an all-time low. Earlier he had scanned her in the crimson dress, had frowned but said nothing. The absence of his admiration, however, had been blatant and from that moment on the red dress had felt like a colossal unflattering mistake. But why was she allowing Mikhail's opinion to matter so much to her? The means to stop the process of what felt like humiliation dead had always been within her own hands and perhaps it was past time that she acted. Her fingers tightened on her envelope purse, which contained her passport. Stas was poised by the exit doors and she walked over to him, her head high, eyes alight with sudden energy again.

'Could you arrange a taxi to take me to the airport?' she asked, knowing she couldn't just walk out and disappear without causing an inexcusable furore.

Momentarily, Stas seemed to freeze. 'Of course,' he told her nonetheless. 'Give me five minutes to organise it.'

Her decision made to fly home as soon as she could get a flight, Kat felt loads happier, as if a giant weight had fallen from her shoulders. She would go home, find a job and somewhere else to live, she reflected as she freshened up in the cloakroom. She didn't *need* to look to Mikhail to do anything for her, certainly not to give her a house she had lost through her own mistakes and done nothing to earn!

When Kat reappeared Stas was waiting to show her through the double exit doors and then he surprised her by throwing open another door off the corridor and she hesitated with a frown. 'Where are you taking me?'

Mikhail filled the doorway like a big dark storm cloud. 'You're not walking out on me.'

Kat settled outraged green eyes on him. *'Watch me!'* she advised.

'We'll discuss it first, *milaya moya,*' Mikhail declared, blocking her path with his tall lean body and pressing the door wider.

Kat supposed she owed him some sort of an explanation. Possibly it had been unrealistic to believe that she could just leave without a confrontation because Mikhail Kusnirovich would never accept anything less blunt. But he didn't own her and she hadn't signed away her life or anything stupid when she signed that wretched agreement with him.

'I'm not your prisoner,' Kat told him, lifting her chin. 'I can leave any time I like—'

'And where are you planning to go at this time of night in a foreign country?' Mikhail demanded harshly.

'I can wait at the airport until there's a flight. I believe the London flights are quite frequent,' Kat pointed out, swallowing so hard in the smouldering silence that her throat muscles ached. In truth she didn't have enough cash in her bank account to pay for a flight home, but she had planned to phone Saffy and ask her sibling to buy a ticket for her.

Mikhail counted slowly and internally to ten but it didn't work any magic on his aggressive mood. The realisation that she was prepared to simply walk out on him had struck him like a punch in the gut and he was genuinely stunned by the concept. A woman had never walked out on him before but he thought it was typical that she would be the first to try and do it. There she stood, her slim figure rigid with resolution, beautiful green eyes defiant and angry, pointed little chin at a combative angle, just daring him to argue. She was as unstable as gelignite, he told himself grimly. Maybe he *should* have paid her more attention in recent days instead of shelving her like a difficult project, he thought furiously, maybe he should have talked to her sooner… but talked to her about what exactly? The number of serious chats Mikhail had enjoyed with women outside business hours couldn't have covered a postage stamp. He didn't do the talking thing; he wasn't in touch with anyone's feelings, least of all his own, and he didn't do serious…which meant there really wasn't much left to talk about.

'I don't want you to leave,' Mikhail spelt out in a harsh undertone, spectacular dark eyes pinned to her with driving tenacity.

'Let's face it…without Stas's warning you, you would barely have noticed my absence,' Kat countered drily. 'You are surrounded by loads of other women tonight—'

'But I don't want any of them,' Mikhail grated without hesitation. 'I want you.'

Kat was grimly amused by that frank admission. 'Then you were going the wrong way about attaining me.'

'There *is* no right way with you. If even you don't know what you want, how am I supposed to deliver it?' he shot at her with stormy impatience.

'I know exactly what I want—I want to go home,' Kat declared, throwing her head back, spiralling russet curls falling back from her heart-shaped face.

'Isn't that just typical of a woman?' Mikhail growled. 'You light a fire and then you run away!'

Outrage rolled through Kat's slender body in an energising wave and she took an angry step forward. 'I am *not* running away!'

'Of course you are,' Mikhail fielded with biting assurance. 'You want me and I want you but evidently you can't cope with something that simple.'

'It's not that simple!' Kat launched back at him furiously, inflamed that he was confidently arguing with her when she was being plunged into ever deeper turmoil.

'It is. You can't handle your own sexual inhibitions. Call yourself a *cougar*?' Mikhail hitched an ebony brow, his derisive amusement unconcealed at the term as applied to her. 'You're more like a toddler in the sex stakes. One step forward, two steps back. If I didn't know there was no malice intended by your behaviour, I'd call you a tease—'

'How dare you?' Kat raked at him, enraged by his censure. 'I warned you that I wouldn't sleep with you!'

'While you continue to respond to my every look and touch,' Mikhail reminded her doggedly. 'You're terrified of having a normal sexual relationship with a man—that's the only reason you're still a virgin!'

'No, it's not!' Kat argued vehemently, high spots of colour burning in her pale cheeks, green eyes raw with rage that he could dare to say such a thing to her when he still didn't know anything about the person she was. 'I refuse to let any man use me for sex the way men used my mother!'

'Your...*mother*?' Mikhail's brows drew together in a frown of incomprehension because, while he might have paid to have an investigative report carried out on Kat, he had paid very little heed to her past. 'What the hell has she got to do with anything?'

Kat blinked rapidly, almost as surprised as he was that she had voiced that comment out loud. It was based on a fear that ran all the way back to her unsettled childhood when Odette had frequently complained that as soon as a man got her into bed, he lost interest in her again. 'I don't want to be used just for my body. Sex is all you're interested in,' Kat protested stiltedly.

Mikhail vaguely appreciated that he had stumbled into one of those 'relationship' talks he always avoided like the plague. Obviously sex was what he was interested in, but what was wrong with that? He had always regarded sex as a normal healthy appetite until he met her and desire became an endurance test.

'I've been used by many women,' he traded with

cool cynicism. 'For sex, for money, for my connections. It happens to all of us. You can't protect yourself from such experiences and it's spineless to run away from them—'

'I'm not spineless!' Yet Kat was starkly disconcerted by his admission that he had also been used by the opposite sex for what he could offer. But she was equally disconcerted by the admission she had made to him and feared that he might be about to make the same deduction that she had for herself. Could she have made it more obvious that she wanted *more* than sex from him? Suddenly she was praying that he didn't think too deeply about what she had said, for the emotions that had urged her to run far and fast in self-defence were too private and new to share with anyone, least of all him.

Scanning her pale taut face, Mikhail expelled his breath in a hiss and strode forward. In a disturbingly sudden movement, he lifted her off her startled feet and ignored her dismayed gasp to settle her down firmly on the leather sofa behind her. 'Sit down and talk to me, then... Tell me what possible influence your mother could still have over you...'

Mikhail felt benevolent as he offered that unparalleled invitation. If it stopped Kat walking out, he would listen to anything, while on another level he was surprisingly keen to know why she gave him so many conflicting messages.

While Kat watched Mikhail open the door to speak to Stas before he sank lithely down opposite her, her mind was already filling with uneasy images. Drinks arrived while she struggled to suppress her unfortunate memories of her childhood. Her mother, Odette, the woman Kat had loved without return until she too became an adult, was someone Kat rarely let herself think about because, even after all this time, Odette's essential indifference to her daughter could still hurt. Odette had always liked to play the victim and, as Odette's biggest audience, Kat had often witnessed more than she should of her mother's tangled love life. Long ago she had buried those distressing memories deep and moved on with her life and it was only now, as she was forced to dig those memories out again, that she appreciated that everything now looked rather different. Reality no longer matched up with the facts, she conceded ruefully. Suddenly she felt exceedingly foolish for not having seen the obvious much sooner.

'Kat.?' Mikhail prompted, surveying her highly expressive face and deeply troubled eyes with frowning force, exasperation clawing at him when they were interrupted by the arrival of the drinks he had ordered.

Kat moistened her lips with the bubbling champagne, grateful for something to hold in her trembling hand. 'My mum, Odette, was a successful model but probably not a very nice person. Our lives were unsettled because her relationships were always breaking down,' she admitted stiffly, reluctant as she was to reveal any vulnerability to him. 'She married my dad for security and then divorced him when her career took off. She deserted the twins' father when he went bankrupt, but still all she ever talked about while I was growing up was how men let *her* down and *used* her. It's only now that I can see that in most cases she was much more of a user than they were.'

Mikhail lowered lush black lashes over his bemused gaze. 'And how does that comparison apply to us?'

'It doesn't,' Kat conceded, ashamed that she had let her mother's self-pitying conditioning influence her outlook without her awareness for so many years. Odette had believed that simply engaging in sex with a man constituted a relationship and that having his baby would make him commit, she reflected wryly, and it was that shallow short-sighted outlook that had ensured that none of her mother's relationships had prospered.

'Do you still want to go back to the UK?'

Her tummy gave an apprehensive lurch as she looked into brilliant dark golden eyes, still the most beautiful she had ever seen in a man's face. He was a very dangerous man, she conceded dizzily, for he had chosen the perfect moment in which to ask that leading question and she could not believe that the timing was accidental. She didn't *want* to leave Mikhail now, she acknowledged guiltily, wasn't yet ready to close the door on what she might still discover about him. Without even realising it, she had been running away, forced into a corner by her mother's brainwashing during her impressionable adolescence and her own terror of being hurt. But logic told her that life was to be lived, mistakes included, and that in any case she was not following her mother's example.

Kat lifted her bright head. 'Not just yet…' she confessed and drained her glass.

'Let's get back on board *Hawk*,' Mikhail urged huskily, as mystified as ever by the strange way in which her mind worked but satisfied by the result. He closed a hand over hers and tugged her up from the sofa.

'What about your guests?'

'They're too busy partying on their own account to notice my absence,' he replied dismissively, long brown fingers tightening resolutely round hers, his breath fanning her cheek as he bent over her. The warm scent of his body tinged with the exclusive cologne he wore infiltrated her. A little quiver of almost painful sexual awareness engulfed her slim length and tensed her muscles.

Kat reddened when she saw Stas study their linked hands but she knew that there wasn't a romantic edge to that connection for Mikhail. No indeed, for once she could read her Russian billionaire's mind. As long as he kept a physical hold of her she couldn't go anywhere he didn't want her to go: he really was that basic. If only she could be as cool-headed and practical as he was, she ruminated worriedly as he tucked her on board the tender that would whisk them out of the harbour and back to the yacht. He had fallen in lust but she was falling in love…

As he pushed open the door of her suite Kat was scarcely breathing from nervous tension and anticipation, but once again he surprised her by stepping back to head for his own accommodation next door.

'Decision time, *milaya moya*,' he quipped, glancing back at her from heavily lidded dark sensual eyes. 'If you want me, you know where to find me.'

CHAPTER EIGHT

KAT LEANT BACK against her door, her heart hammering inside her chest… *You know where to find me.*

On the other side of the door she had locked. Could she really blame him for telling her to take the initiative for a change? She had made such a deal over *not* sleeping with Mikhail and, without ever meaning to be unfair, she had allowed him to touch her and then had withdrawn that licence at the last possible moment. But then right from the first minute she had laid eyes on Mikhail Kusnirovich, she had wanted him, wanted him more than she had ever thought she could want any man, and, unhappily for both of them, desire had decimated her common sense and control.

And common sense and control, Kat recognised, had absolutely nothing to do with the way she felt about Mikhail. Desire was a much more primitive feeling it was an unquenchable craving that it literally hurt to deny. With impatient hands she shed the green dress and her underwear and left her clothing lying in a heap, defying her instinctive urge to put every item tidily away. For too long she had lived by a rigid set of rules and she had questioned nothing. Instead she had blindly obeyed those rules like an obedient little girl.

Now all of a sudden she was looking back at the last

conservative decade of her life and she was finally *done* with playing safe and even more sick of always trying to do the right thing to set a good example! What gains had her good example achieved? It hadn't stopped Emmie from getting pregnant outside marriage any more than it had stopped Emmie's twin, Saffy, from getting married and divorced too young.

But it was still that conviction that she had to set a good example that had ensured that Kat hadn't had a man in her life for more years than she cared to recall. How dared Mikhail call her a coward? Cowardice had had nothing to do with it! There had been no arbitrary decision to remain a virgin. Instead she had consciously chosen to put her sisters' need for stability ahead of her own needs as a woman.

But would it really have damaged her siblings so much had she enjoyed intimacy with a lover? Now her sisters were moving on, making their own lives and leaving her behind, still ridiculously ignorant for a woman of her age. Continuing such self-denial was pointless. It really didn't matter if she only slept with Mikhail to satisfy her curiosity about sex, she thought painfully. It didn't even matter if she loved him and hoped for more than she would ever receive from him. A mistake was a mistake and not a disaster, and she was strong enough to survive making mistakes. Never again would she run away from the unknown like a frightened child or use her mother's errors of judgement as her safety valve.

Clad in a gossamer-thin silk nightgown, Kat unlocked the door between her suite and the master suite to push it wide with an unsteady hand. Mikhail appeared in the bathroom doorway, only a towel linked round his lean bronzed hips. His black diamond eyes settled on

her and a smile of satisfaction instantly curved his wide
sensual mouth. Half naked he was an imposing sight,
his black hair spiky and damp from the shower, water
droplets scattered across his powerful hair-roughened
pecs and rock-hard abdominal muscles. He had a fabulous body, she acknowledged helplessly, and her face
coloured as she tried very hard not to stare at his potent male perfection.

'I feel as though I've been waiting for you for ever,'
Mikhail husked, moving forward to scoop her up in his
arms and settle her down on the wide divan bed.

'And I can't believe I'm here,' Kat confided jerkily.

'Believe, *moyo zolotse.*' His mouth swooped down
on hers in a kiss as evocative as rough velvet brushing
her parted lips, his tongue spearing between and tangling with her own. The intoxicating taste of him was
more than enough to chase the goose bumps of nervous tension from her skin and she shivered helplessly
against him. Her fingers curved to his broad brown
shoulders while damp heat surged between her thighs
and she could feel her breasts swelling, the nipples tingling as she pushed the sensitive mounds into the hard
muscular wall of his chest. Even through the thickness
of the towel she could feel the hard wedge of his erection against her thigh and she trembled at the thought
of him pushing inside her to sate the tormenting ache
stirring in her pelvis.

He pulled back, remarkably beautiful eyes skimming
her hectically flushed face while his hands roamed over
her silk-clad curves, cupping her breasts before rising
to slide down the straps on her shoulders and bare her
tender flesh. The gown slid to her waist and he captured her distended nipples between finger and thumb

and tugged to send arrows of longing shooting down into her groin.

'Mikhail…' She was breathless, quivering, almost frightened by the powerful surges of response assailing her.

'Your breasts are so sensitive that I want to torture you with pleasure,' Mikhail growled.

His mouth captured a rosy beaded tip and she gasped, jerking at the response that travelled straight down to heat her pelvis and making no protest as he lowered her down against the pillows. With his tongue and the edges of his teeth he played with the engorged buds while easing the nightie from round her hips to cast it aside. In the lamp light the porcelain purity of her slender figure glowed like polished alabaster. Big hands cupped her hips, parted her thighs and traced a trail to the silken heart of her where she was so desperately wet and swollen.

Pure undiluted hunger fired Mikhail's eyes and he pulled lithely back from her to draw her down towards the foot of the bed. She was limp with surprise and uncertainty, tensing when he pushed her knees apart and freezing into rigidity when he spread her wide to expose that part of her that she usually kept hidden. 'What are you doing?' she demanded strickenly.

'Trust me…relax,' Mikhail soothed. 'I want tonight to be the best night you've ever had with a man—'

'It'll be the only night,' she reminded him shakily while she fought the urge to snap her thighs shut like scissors and blanked her overpowering awareness that she was naked and exposed.

'Not *our* only night,' Mikhail forecast with confidence. 'But I'll make it good, *moyo zolotse*…'

'Promises, promises…' Her voice shook uncontrollably as she dared to voice that sally.

He sank his hands below her hips to lift her and his tongue swiped across her clitoris. That instant pleasure was almost too intense to be borne and her hands clawed convulsively into the bedding beneath her as he teased her tender flesh. She tried very hard to swallow back the noises rising in her throat but his unnerving skill at heightening her responses made that an impossible challenge. Her back arched, her hips rose and she cried out as his fingers penetrated her in the way she most needed to be touched, giving her just a little of what she helplessly craved. She went out of control so fast then that she had no idea of what was happening to her. She was shaking, alternately rigid and then weak before the great surge of irresistible pleasure shockwaved through her with almost brutal force and she was crying out and splintering and shuddering with the intensity of her climax.

Blinded by that all-encompassing pleasure, she looked up into his face and he gazed down at her through a veil of thick dark lashes as flattering as a fringe of ebony lace and muttered hungrily, 'I love watching you come…'

Her face burned and she tensed as he rose over her and she felt his bold shaft ease into her. He was thick and amazingly hard and he felt like an incredibly tight fit while her muscles slowly stretched to accommodate his size. His groan of uninhibited pleasure sent a jolt of delight darting through her. The raw tension in his lean, powerful muscles told her of the care and control he was exerting, but there was no escape from the brief but sharp sting of pain that assailed her when he sank deeper into her and broke through the final barrier of her innocence.

'I'm sorry,' Mikhail growled, stunning black diamond eyes glittering with the raw excitement he could not hide. 'I was trying not to hurt you.'

'It's all right… It's not hurting any more,' Kat confided, lifting her hips up to him in an instinctive movement and moaning as he drove deep into her again.

'You feel so good I don't think I could stop,' Mikhail groaned, pulling out of her receptive body and then plunging back into her hot slick depths again with a rough growl of satisfaction.

He taught her that rhythm very quickly and the constant physical stimulation fed into the overwhelming excitement he had unleashed. Her slim body rose below his again, her eyes like stars as the ripples of her second orgasm pulsed through them both, so that he drove even harder into her and shuddered over her with a shout of satisfaction he could not restrain.

Her heart was thumping so fast that even lying down she felt dizzy and breathless and utterly unlike her usual sane and sensible self. Her arms closed round him. 'Is it always that exciting?' she whispered shyly.

Mikhail pinned her to his hot damp body. 'Rarely. It's the best sex I've ever had, *milaya moya.*'

And for a split second she was pleased by the compliment and the overpowering sense of intimacy that she was enjoying while she lay in his arms. But the feeling of peace and relaxation didn't last once she thought about the label of having given him the best sex he'd ever had. Somehow instead of making her feel complimented that made her feel cheap, as if she had supplied just another novelty experience to a male who had already enjoyed a wide variety of experiences in the field of sex.

'Time for a shower,' he breathed, rolling her to the side of the bed with him and urging her in the direction of the bathroom.

Her legs felt as collapsible as a deckchair's and she clung to a muscular male arm, wincing when she felt the dulled ache at the heart of her.

'You're sore…' Mikhail husked, studying her expressive face, laughing when she blushed crimson. 'Well, what did you expect?'

'I should go back to my room,' Kat muttered, pulling back from the big tiled wall he was about to step around.

'No, I want you to stay,' Mikhail confided, hauling her up against his big powerful body as he switched on the water.

'Thought you liked your privacy,' Kat reminded him tautly, disconcerted by the amount of intimacy being forced on her all at once, uneasy with her nakedness below the strong overhead lights.

'But I like the thought of you in my bed first thing in the morning even more,' Mikhail growled against her throat as he pinned her to the tiled wall, dropped his hands to her hips to hold her there and crushed her lush mouth with hungry urgency beneath his.

Imprisoned by his big powerful body, Kat couldn't breathe for excitement and she discovered that even the tenderness between her thighs couldn't stop her wanting him again with a level of hunger that shook her. 'Now my hair's wet,' she complained prosaically.

'You'll survive,' Mikhail breathed, letting his tongue delve between her lips in an urgent rhythmic foray that mimicked the act of intercourse so closely that she quivered with spellbound yearning, the distended tips of her breasts grazing his hard pectoral muscles. Against her stomach she could feel him rigid and urgent again and she marvelled at his speedy recovery.

And Kat, who never would have dreamt of going to bed with wet hair forgot about her hair, and forgot to worry about what it would look like the next morning. In the grip of passion, Mikhail was too determined to withstand. He strode from the shower with her wrapped round him and seated her on the granite vanity counter. It was the work of a moment for him to snatch a contraceptive from a drawer, tear the packet open and don a condom. He stepped between her spread legs to ease into her honeyed softness again with a sigh of profound relief.

'Thought you were going to wait until tomorrow,' Kat reminded him, her teeth gritting on a spasm of erotic pleasure so devouring it resembled pain because he was being extraordinarily cautious and gentle and slow. Little tremors of exquisite excitement made her clench tight around him.

'Never was any good at waiting,' Mikhail growled, fighting to stay in control as he rocked against her, fearful of hurting her but wanting her so desperately it was like a mounting fever in his blood.

The ball of his thumb circled the little nub of nerve-endings at the swollen heart of her and she moaned wildly under his mouth, her arms tightening round him, her nails digging into his shoulders as he quickened the pace of his possession.

In the morning he took her again, his mouth tracing the corded delicacy of her throat to awaken her before he sank his thickness into her receptive body over and over again until she screamed her explosive release into the pillow beneath her head.

'Shower with me,' he urged afterwards.

Kat knew he wasn't to be trusted in the shower and reluctantly laughed. 'I'll use my own.'

'Breakfast in ten minutes,' he told her firmly.

Kat didn't move until he had vanished safely into his bathroom. The ache of overindulgence was so strong that she gritted her teeth when she got out of bed and returned to her own room to freshen up. A cry of horror was wrenched from her when she looked in a mirror and saw her curls all standing on end in a wall of frizz. She looked like a rag doll who had been tortured. With no time to do anything with her recalcitrant curls, she scraped the messy russet torrent back and secured her tumbled hair with a clip. Showered, she dabbed on a little light make-up, trying to conceal the swollen contours of her mouth and the evidence of his stubble marking her with a beard rash across her cheeks and throat. She pulled on underwear and yanked a sundress from the dressing room, hurrying because she knew he was so impatient that he would come looking for her if she didn't appear on time.

So *that* was sex, she reflected in a daze, so much more than she had expected: more exciting, more intimate, more everything really. And she had loved everything he had done to her, had swiftly got over her shyness and uncertainty to appreciate that he was a good lover and that she was lucky to have had so considerate and skilled an introduction to intimacy. But now she was wondering if she had lived up to *his* expectations or whether at the end of the day he could be wondering what all the fuss had been about.

Breakfast was served on the extensive private deck beyond Mikhail's suite. Sunlight glancing off the turquoise waters of the Mediterranean sea, Kat sipped her coffee and tried to stop smiling, indeed to cram a lid down on the bubbling happiness welling up inside her. Happiness wasn't fitting. They didn't have a relationship for her to celebrate or pin hopes on. All they had was an affair and now that they were actually having an affair that agreement they had made had to become history, Kat thought ruefully.

'You can't give me the farmhouse back now,' Kat told Mikhail squarely.

An ebony brow quirked. 'Why not?'

'It would be inappropriate now that we're sleeping together,' Kat pointed out flatly as she took a seat.

'According to whose book of sexual etiquette?' Mikhail queried very drily.

'If I accepted the house back now, it would be like accepting payment for sex—'

'Don't look for trouble where none exists. I don't offer payment for sex, never have, never will.'

'I wouldn't feel comfortable now letting you return the house to me,' Kat explained stubbornly.

'Tough,' Mikhail remarked, unimpressed. 'We made that agreement and I see no reason to deviate from it. That house is your home.'

'That house belongs to you now,' Kat retorted in crisp disagreement.

Mikhail vented a sound of exasperation. '*Zatk'nis!* Shut up!' he told her impatiently. 'You're talking nonsense.'

Her green eyes flared. 'Think about what I'm saying... You know it makes sense!'

'But I'm not listening,' Mikhail responded with an

imperious shift of a lean brown hand that dismissed the
discussion in its entirety.

Her teeth gnashed together.

'I tell you what to do…you *do* it,' Mikhail drawled
softly. 'That was also in the agreement and I wouldn't
like you to lose that talent now.'

Sheer frustration sent Kat up out of her seat again
and she rested her slender forearms on the rail to stare
out to sea. 'You sound like a Neanderthal again.'

Strong hands skimmed down her spine to curve
down over her hips. 'Whatever turns you on—'

'*That* doesn't,' she told him succinctly.

Long fingers inched up her skirt and glided up the
silken length of her thigh and she froze. 'What the heck
are you doing?' she exclaimed in consternation.

Masculine fingertips flirted with the lacy edge of
the knickers interrupting his exploration. 'Take them
off,' he said.

'Of course I'm not taking them off!' Kat protested
in disbelief. 'Have you gone insane?'

'Just the thought of you naked below that dress excites me,' Mikhail purred, pressing his lips to a delicate
spot just below her ear in a caress that left her hot and
breathlessly eager for more. 'What's wrong with that?'

'I wouldn't feel right without them on,' Kat muttered
tautly while shamelessly angling her head back to provide easier access for his wide sensual mouth.

In answer, Mikhail hauled her up against him and
kissed her with a hungry fervour that thoroughly unsettled her. With her cradled in his arms he sank down into
his seat with her again, long caressing fingers stroking
her slim thighs below the skirt of her dress. Recognising that he really didn't know how to take no for an
answer but simply pursued another path when he met

with opposition, Kat slapped a hand down on the hem of her dress to prevent it from rising any further and to restrict his clever hands. 'No,' she told him flatly. 'I'm keeping my underwear on!'

'You're so stubborn,' Mikhail growled in complaint against her lush mouth.

'You're even worse,' Kat complained, idle fingers brushing through his luxuriant black hair while her languorous gaze admired the exotic slash of his cheekbones, the arrogant jut of his nose and the strength of his jaw line. 'But luckily for you, you're also incredibly sexy...'

Mikhail tilted his imperious dark head back and laughed out loud. 'Am I?'

Barely able to credit that she could already be so relaxed in his company that she could tease him, Kat grinned. 'I think so...but shouldn't we be joining your guests for a farewell breakfast?'

'Stop being so sensible,' Mikhail urged with a frown.

'I'm *always* sensible,' Kat told him ruefully.

'If you were that sensible you would have avoided me like the plague,' Mikhail asserted with conviction.

And that he could coolly issue that warning sent a cold shiver down Kat's vulnerable spine. It was sex, only sex, that had brought them together, she reminded herself urgently, nothing more involved or dangerous. He was fantastic in bed and that was that: she didn't *have* any other feelings for him. No, not one single tender feeling or stab of womanly curiosity, she reflected, and on that soothing thought she dragged her fingers out of his hair and shifted off his lap as though someone had harpooned her with a flaming arrow. After all, she didn't want to give him the impression that he was sleeping with a clinging vine.

* * *

'My mother died when I was six years old,' Mikhail admitted grudgingly.

'What did she die of?' Kat prompted, ignoring the I-don't-want-to-talk-about-this signals he was emanating in a defensive force field. He never ever mentioned his family or his childhood and, considering that he knew everything there was to know about her, his determined reticence was starting to annoy her.

'Being pregnant. She went into labour at home. Something went wrong and she bled to death. The baby died as well,' Mikhail spelt out grimly.

'That must have been very traumatic for you and your father,' Kat said quietly, disconcerted by the tragedy he had revealed.

'If she'd had proper medical attention, she probably would have survived but my father didn't want her going into hospital.'

Her brow furrowed. 'Why not?'

Lean, darkly handsome features taut, his black diamond eyes glittered and his handsome mouth compressed into a hard line of dissatisfaction. 'I don't want to talk about this. It's not my favourite topic of conversation…*vy menya panimayete*…do you understand me?' he bit out with harsh emphasis, swinging round and striding away.

Kat suppressed a sigh. Three weeks of unparalleled exposure to Mikhail had taught her that she apparently had the tact of an elephant in hobnail boots. She was no good at pussyfooting round the things he didn't want to discuss. Indeed the minute she realised he was holding back on her that topic became what she most wanted him to talk about. Secrets nagged at her. What was wrong with curiosity? Surely it was natural for her to be curious?

The problem was that in recent weeks she had begun to feel misleadingly close to Mikhail. They had spent so much time together. Another party of guests had come and gone midway through the cruise. Barbecues had been staged on deserted beaches, trips organised to exclusive clubs and designer shops. He had complimented her on her skills as a hostess but she hadn't had to make much of an effort. She liked meeting different people and loved to ensure that they enjoyed themselves and relaxed. After all, those same traits had once persuaded her to open a guest house. But on a more personal level she could not afford to forget that the man who slept beside her all night long was only a lover and not a partner. There were limits to their relationship and evidently she had just breached them and caused offence. Unfortunately for her, she was continually battling the desire to break down Mikhail's reserve.

In the office on the upper deck, Mikhail opened his laptop. Kat would sleep in her own bed tonight. He could get along without her for one night. He had never been dependent on a woman in his life and she was no different. Well, she was different in one aspect: he wasn't tired of her yet, hadn't yet had enough of that slender, soft-skinned body of hers that melted into his as if she had been created to be his perfect fit. Sex was amazing with her, everything he had ever wanted, everything he had never dreamt he might find with one woman. The pulse at his groin stirred, the stubborn flesh swelling and hardening behind his zip even at the thought of her. Three weeks and she was *still* turning him on hard and fast. He didn't like it—he resented her power over him, loathed it when she tried to plunge him into the kind of meaningful dialogue he never had with women. In a sudden movement he snapped the laptop shut again and rose lithely upright, six feet five inches of power-fully frustrated and aggressive male.

'Where is she?' he asked Stas, who was hovering by the door.

'Still out on deck,' the older man confirmed.

He found Kat leaning against the rail looking out to sea, her dress fluttering against her slim curves in the breeze. His hands came down on her shoulders and she jerked in surprise.

'Stop snooping,' Mikhail told her, tugging her back into the hard heat of his big body.

'I wasn't snooping!' Kat argued vehemently without turning her head. 'I'm not a snoop!'

'My childhood wasn't exactly a bowl of cherries,' Mikhail breathed curtly.

'Neither was mine but you accept that and move on...'

'I don't think about it, so there's nothing to move on from, *milaya moya*.' Mikhail pressed her up against the rail and buried his mouth hungrily in the soft sensitive curve of flesh where her neck joined her shoulder. She shivered, imprisoned by his body, achingly aware of her own and the hunger he could ignite so easily.

'The fact you don't think about it and won't talk about it says it all,' Kat quipped. 'Why all the secrecy?'

'I have no secrets,' Mikhail fielded.

And not for one moment did Kat believe that claim, for he was a fascinatingly complex man, who revealed very little about himself on a personal level.

'My mother was from a tribe of nomadic herders in Siberia,' he volunteered with startling abruptness. 'My father was trying to buy up oil and gas rights in the region when he saw her. He said it was love at first sight. She was very beautiful but she didn't speak a word of Russian and she was illiterate—'

'It sounds very romantic to me,' Kat said defiantly.

'He had to marry her before her family would let her go. He took her from life in a herders' tent and put her in a mansion. He was obsessed with her. He enjoyed the fact that she had to depend on him for everything, that she understood nothing about the life he led or the world he lived in as a wealthy businessman. He liked her ignorance, her subservience,' Mikhail breathed scathingly. 'He never took her out. Behind closed doors, he treated her like a domestic slave and when she got things wrong he beat the hell out of her!'

Kat twisted round and focused stricken green eyes on his lean, strong face. 'Did he beat you as well?'

'Only when I tried to protect her,' Mikhail replied, his handsome mouth twisting at the recollection. 'I was only six when she died, so I might have got in his way a few times but I wasn't physically capable of preventing him from hurting her. He suffered from violent rages yet she worshipped the ground he walked on because she didn't know any better. She thought it was her duty to make her husband happy and if he wasn't happy she believed it was her fault.'

'It was probably the way she was raised. It's hard to shake that kind of conditioning,' Kat muttered soothingly, sensing the pain that he refused to express. There had been violence in his childhood. He had loved and pitied his mother and had been powerless to help her. She could imagine the wound of regret and frustration that that must have engraved on his soul.

'You fight me every step of the way,' Mikhail pointed out.

'Maybe you would have preferred a subservient woman—'

'*No!*' The interruption was harsh, unequivocal. 'I wouldn't want you if you were scared of me or always trying to impress or please me.'

'I never really understood why you do want me,' Kat murmured truthfully.

Mikhail flipped her round and stared down at her with smouldering dark eyes. 'You don't need to understand.'

Long fingers were gently smoothing her upper arms, awakening her to the hunger she couldn't restrain. He mightn't scare her but the hunger *did*. It overpowered her will, made her desperate and needy, two things she always hid from him. Even now, when he simply looked at her, arousal ran like a current of fire through her body as her breasts swelled and peaked and liquid heat curled between her thighs.

'I want you now, *moyo zolotse,*' he husked and the dark rough edge of his voice slid over her senses like silk.

'Because I upset you—'

'I wasn't upset—'

Her winged brows arched in disbelief at the claim. 'You were furious!'

An appreciative laugh was wrenched from Mikhail. His face etched with amusement. He really was a breathtakingly handsome man, she conceded dizzily. He pulled her up against him, fingertips brushing a slender thigh as he lifted her skirt.

'I was about to say that you'll never make diplomatic status but perhaps I was wrong. You're bare and you know how much I like that.' Mikhail breathed a little raggedly as he scooped her off her feet and carried her back indoors.

Her face was burning with colour. She was a shameless hussy who rarely wore a full set of underwear in his radius. Three weeks as this man's lover had changed her and she didn't think she could ever go back to the prim and cautious woman she had been before. Although she was always waiting to see him betray some sign of boredom or lack of interest, he never seemed to get enough of her.

He settled her down on the bed and stood over her, ripping off his shirt to expose the six-pack abs that she so admired and unzipping his chino pants to reveal a very healthy erection. She reached out to touch him, stroking his thick hardness with gentle fingers, watching his eyes narrow below his lush lashes and shimmer with unashamed desire. He came down on top of her and kissed her with hungry driving urgency, his tongue stabbing between her parted with lips with an erotic skill.

He wasn't prepared to free her for long enough to remove her dress in the proper fashion and as he attempted to impatiently extract her from its folds fabric ripped and she gasped, 'Mikhail! I liked this dress—'

With a stifled curse he concluded the struggle by pulling it over her head and finally flung it aside. '*Ti takaya valnuyishaya*...you are so exciting. I can't wait—'

'We only got out of bed a couple of hours ago,' Kat reminded him, swiping the tip of her tongue over his wide full lower lip, loving the scent and the taste of him.

'Obviously you should have given me more attention while we were there,' Mikhail quipped speciously, his hands cupping the soft full mounds of her breasts and rubbing her straining pink nipples, so that her breath caught in her throat and the smart answer on the tip of her tongue got lost somewhere in the passage from her brain.

Her eyes drifted closed as he kissed her again and stroked between her legs. She quivered, hips rising as he pleasured her with consummate sizzling ease, touching her where she needed to be touched, setting alight every nerve ending in her writhing body until an uncontrollable ache built at the heart of her.

'You're so hot and tight,' Mikhail growled against her throat, pushing back from her to close his hands round her waist and turn her over onto her stomach. 'I need you now.'

He tugged up her hips and sank into her in one long deep thrust that made her cry out in shock and delight. Her level of pleasure went into overload as he took her hard and fast. Intense sensation laced with wild excitement seized hold of her. The slam of his body into hers kicked off a chain reaction of spellbinding heat in her pelvis. The excitement surged to an unbearable level and she was gasping, whimpering, begging until the skilled brush of his thumb over her clitoris sent her rocketing into a blazing paradise of erotic pleasure that splintered through her quivering length like an explosion. She collapsed down on the bed as he groaned his own release into her shoulder.

'You're crushing me,' she protested, struggling desperately to catch her breath again.

Mikhail expelled his breath and released her from his weight, rolling onto the bed beside her before pulling her back into his arms to kiss her with lingering appreciation. 'You set me on fire,' he muttered thickly. 'But the moment I stop I only want to do it again—'

'Forget it...I won't be capable of moving again this side of midnight,' Kat mumbled, her body still pulsing and thrumming from the intensity of her climax, her limbs resting so heavily on the mattress that they felt like iron weights.

'I'm ready and willing to do all the work.' But then, in a disconcertingly sudden movement, Mikhail fell back from her and swore in Russian. 'I didn't use a condom!'

Consternation gripped Kat. She sat up, seriously startled by that admission, for he never took risks in that department. No matter when or where they made love he was always careful to use contraception to protect her. Being in a relationship where pregnancy could even be a risk was, however, still so new and surprising to Kat that her mind refused to even estimate the possibility of an unplanned pregnancy.

'And if my calculations are correct we may have chosen a bad day to be careless,' Mikhail breathed tautly, his strong jaw line hardening at the prospect. 'Less than two weeks have passed since your last period, which puts us slap bang in the middle of your fertile phase.'

His intimate grasp of the workings of her female body embarrassed Kat, but there was no hiding such facts in a relationship such as theirs. 'But I'm at an age where my fertility is probably going downhill,' she told him thinly, not really wanting to be reminded of that possibility but keen to stop him worrying.

'These days lots of women are giving birth in their forties,' Mikhail fielded drily. 'I doubt that you have any grounds to assume that you're infertile.'

'Well, let's hope we don't have cause to find out

whether I am or not,' Kat muttered ruefully, sliding off the bed and heading into the bathroom because all of a sudden she needed a moment alone and unobserved.

The Kat she saw reflected in the mirror was all shaken up, her eyes dazed, her face pale and troubled. An affair seemed trouble free until the real world threatened and there could be nothing more real world than an accidental pregnancy. For goodness' sake, her sister Emmie was pregnant and hadn't she disapproved, deemed her irresponsible and feared for her sibling's future? How much less excuse did she have at her age? She should have taken care of birth control even before she got on the yacht. Better safe than sorry should have been her guiding principle. She had been so sure she wouldn't end up in Mikhail's bed and where had that belief got her?

Mikhail joined her in the shower. He ran a reproving fingertip along the anxious line of her compressed lips. 'Stop worrying about it. If you conceive, we'll handle it together. We're not frightened teenagers,' he pointed out levelly.

But the day after tomorrow she would be leaving the yacht and he would no longer be part of her life. He had said nothing to make her think otherwise and she preferred that. She didn't want him promising to phone and then not bothering. She had fallen in love with him but that wasn't his fault. He had made her no promises and told her no lies. So, how had she managed to fall for him?

Was it when he first ensured that she got her favourite chocolate breakfast drink every morning even though he thought it was a disgustingly sweet concoction? When he started teaching her simple words of Russian? When he tolerated her obsession with a certain television reality show and let her watch it even though it bored him to death? Or was it when he most unexpectedly ran her a hot bath when she found herself suffering one evening from embarrassing cramps? Or even when he treated her as though she was the only woman in the world for him, angling his head down to catch her every word, offering advice on the way she handled her sisters, telling her where she had gone wrong with her guest house? No, Mikhail's full attention was not all a source of joy, she conceded with wry amusement, for he thought he knew everything and that there was no problem he could not fix.

Sometimes she lay awake in bed beside him, studying his lean bronzed profile and the black lashes almost hitting his spectacular cheekbones, and she would try to remember what life had been like without him. Unhappily for her, she didn't want to remember that time or the absence of fun and passion that had made her life so colourless and predictable. Life was never that predictable in Mikhail's radius. It shocked her that she could have lived so many years without ever discovering such joy and delight in another person.

CHAPTER NINE

'WHAT DO YOU want to do today?' Mikhail prompted Kat the following morning as he wrapped a fleecy towel round her dripping figure.

'I thought you had work to do—'

'On your *last* day?' A black brow slashed up.

Her heart thudded as though he had pulled a knife on her, dismay reverberating through her slender body. She had actually thought he might not be aware that the month and the agreed amount of time was up. What a fool she had been! Clearly he had an internal calendar every bit as accurate as her own and it was a timely reminder that she had something she really did need to discuss with him *before* they parted.

'Could we be ordinary people for a change?' she heard herself ask, thinking that it would be easier to talk to him away from the yacht as he was highly unlikely to stage a row with her in a public place.

'Ordinary?' he queried blankly.

'Walk down a street without an escort that attracts attention, window-shop, go for coffee some place that isn't fancy...' she extended uncertainly. 'Simple things.'

Dark as night eyes widening in surprise at the request, Mikhail shrugged a broad shoulder. 'I'm sure I can manage that.'

The tender dropped them at the boarded promenade walk that skirted the coastline of the resort. Stas and his companions followed them but kept their distance. Casually clad in shorts and an open-necked shirt, Mikhail urged her into the town and, closing a hand over hers, he walked her down the main street. She checked out shop windows and went into a gift shop where she insisted on paying for a small glass owl that she knew Topsy would happily add to her collection.

'I've decided I don't like independent women,' Mikhail imparted, watching her study a display of sparkling dress rings in a jeweller's window. 'There's nothing here worthy of your interest... At those prices it's all fake.'

'I'm not a snob—'

'I am,' Mikhail interposed without hesitation. 'Which one do you like?'

'The green one,' she confided, surprised he had asked.

'I couldn't bear to look at that on your finger,' Mikhail derided and he tugged her on down the busy street at a smart pace. 'Where are we going for coffee?'

Kat picked a quiet outdoor café set above the beach with comfortable seats and a beautiful view of the sea. A resigned look on his strong face, Mikhail folded his big powerful frame down into a chair that creaked alarmingly. 'So what's so exciting about coming here?' he enquired, keen for her to spell out the source of the attraction.

'That's the point. It's not exciting or fancy, it's just plain and peaceful,' she told him lightly, knowing she had a thorny subject to broach before she departed and wanting to get that little discussion over and done with somewhere where Mikhail was unlikely to lose his cool.

Kat was so far removed from his usual style of lover that his fascination with her was understandable, Mikhail conceded impatiently, striving tolerantly not to frown with disapproval as she sipped at yet another sickeningly sweet chocolate drink, which could only be bad for her health. Didn't she care about her well-being? Or the fact that she was currently as poor as a church mouse? Any other woman he had slept with would, at the very least, have thought nothing of marching him out to some designer retail outlet so that he could reward her generously for her time with the goodbye gift of a new wardrobe…

So, it had finally come: the moment to say goodbye. He would miss Kat, he acknowledged reluctantly, and not only in bed. He would miss her ability to challenge him, her refusal to be impressed by what his money could buy, even her easy friendliness with his staff and his guests, although he would not miss her ridiculous obsession with reality shows that portrayed a lifestyle that ironically she appeared to have no interest in acquiring for herself. And missing a woman, even rating a woman as being capable of giving him more than a few weeks of amusement, was not a familiar experience for Mikhail. He had always believed that for every woman he left behind another even more appealing would soon appear and experience had borne out that trusty conviction. He would move on as he always did, of course he would.

And no doubt she would move on quickly as well, he reflected darkly, for he was convinced that Lorne would track her down once he knew that Mikhail had ditched her. Lorne Arnold had been very taken with Kat… Lorne was waiting in the wings ready to pounce. Mikhail gritted his teeth, trying not to imagine Kat in bed with Lorne, parting those wonderfully long legs for him and making those throaty little cries when she climaxed. He felt sick to the stomach. But why should that imagery bother him so much? He wasn't possessive about women, never had been, wasn't sensitive either. When it was over, it was over. He wasn't unstable and irrational like his father, the sort of man who obsessed over one special irreplaceable woman and drank himself to death when she was gone. He didn't *do* emotion, he didn't get attached…or hurt or disappointed either. That was the bottom line: he never ever made himself vulnerable. That was a risk that only the foolish ran and he had never been a fool.

'What are you thinking about?' Kat prompted, having noted the grim set of his strong jawline and the flinty hardness of his eyes as he gazed out to sea. 'You look angry.'

'Why would I be angry?' Mikhail enquired, irritated that she watched him so closely and read him so accurately. She got under his skin in some way and wrecked his self-control. Only a few hours had passed since he had forgotten to use a condom for the first time in his life but that single little instant of shocking forgetfulness had shattered his equilibrium. How could any woman excite him that much? He needed a little distance from her; he *needed* to send her home for his own peace of mind.

'I don't know but you certainly don't look happy,' Kat remarked gingerly, picking up on his irritation as well. She would never work out what made Mikhail tick. She did recognise that he had a dark side, a core he never exposed, but he was not, as a rule, moody or bad-tempered. Quick-tempered, yes, bad-tempered, no.

'I'm fine,' Mikhail insisted while mentally engaged

in drawing up a list of what he *didn't* like about Kat. She asked awkward questions and refused to back off even when he made his dissatisfaction clear. She snuggled up to him in bed, which was actually rather endearing, he conceded grudgingly. He might not be a touchy-feely kind of guy, but he did not find the natural warmth and affection she showed him objectionable in any way. On the other hand, she liked the shower a lot hotter than he did and also liked to eat disgustingly sweet things— were those flaws too petty to consider? Since when had he been petty? Since when had he had to think of reasons why he should ditch a woman? He would buy her a fabulous jewel to show his appreciation. He dug out his mobile phone to make the arrangements.

Kat sighed the minute she saw the phone in his lean hand. 'Is that call really necessary?' she asked gently.

Recognising the reproof for what it was, Mikhail ground his teeth together and added another score to her tally of flaws. '*Da*...it is.'

Kat nodded, wishing his mind weren't always one hundred per cent focused on business. Was it naive of her to have hoped that he would let his guard down a little on her last day and engage in meaningful conversation? Mentally she winced at that pathetic hope. Had she really thought Mikhail might come over all romantic and tell her that he wanted her to extend her stay? What a silly dream that would be for her to cherish when she badly needed to go home and pack up her belongings in the farmhouse! After all, Emmie had already established that a little terraced house in the village would soon be available for rent. It wasn't like Kat to be so impractical and it was past time that she told Mikhail what she had decided about Birkside. She studied his bold bronzed profile while he talked on his phone and her eyes warmed, any prospect of practicality draining away. She adored those eyelashes, thick as fly swats, the only softening element in his lean dark face. But there was more to her feelings than the fact that he was an incredibly handsome man and a breathtakingly passionate and exciting lover. She loved his strong work ethic, his open-handed generosity for the right charitable cause, his bluntness, his essentially liberal outlook.

'We have something to talk about,' Kat said stiffly.

'We can talk when we get back on board,' Mikhail murmured abstractedly as he dug his phone back in his pocket.

'You want to leave already? You haven't even touched your coffee yet,' Kat pointed out.

'There's a chip in the cup,' Mikhail informed her drily. 'I don't do ordinary very well...I'm sorry.'

In a forgiving mood, Kat shrugged a narrow shoulder. 'That's OK. You're not on trial. I do need to talk about that legal agreement we made though—'

Mikhail frowned. 'That's water under the bridge—'

'No, it's not. I can't accept the house from you now,' she said with a tight little grimace of discomfiture. 'In the circumstances it would feel too much like payment for services rendered in the bedroom.'

'Don't be ridiculous!' Mikhail told her bluntly. 'I offered the house and you accepted it—it's a done deal.'

'I haven't accepted it and I'm not going to,' Kat protested stubbornly. 'The house is worth thousands and thousands of pounds and far too big a payment for the amount of hostessing I've done for you.'

'That's my decision, not yours,' Mikhail traded curtly, dark eyes now cool as rain on her sun-warmed skin; indeed she actually felt physically chilled by that look.

Kat's spine was rigid with tension but she was determined not to surrender because for once she knew that she was right and he was wrong. 'I won't accept you signing the house back to me. I've thought about this and I mean what I'm saying, Mikhail. Everything's changed between us since we made that agreement and it would be wrong to stick to it.'

Mikhail thrust back his chair and sprang upright to stare down at her with intimidatingly cold, dark and angry eyes. 'You're getting your house back…*end of*!' he framed with a growling edge of ferocity.

Out of the corner of her eye she watched Stas rush to pay the bill while simultaneously keeping a wary eye trained on his employer. She reddened when she saw the diners at the next table staring at them.

Kat hurried over to Mikhail's side before he could stride off without her. 'I had to tell you how I felt,' she told him ruefully.

'And now you know how *I* feel,' he countered grimly. 'Stop messing me around, Kat! It annoys the hell out of me!'

'I'm not doing that,' Kat protested in sharp disconcertion.

But that they had differing opinions on that score was clear when the tender whisked them back to *The Hawk* and Mikhail strode away from her the minute they boarded. She had said what she had to say and she was not taking it back, she told herself squarely, and she went downstairs to her suite to pack her case so that she would be ready to leave in the morning. She walked next door into Mikhail's suite to retrieve her wrap, two nightdresses and the toiletries that had taken up residence in his bathroom. When she returned to her own room, she was taken aback to find Mikhail lodged in the doorway like a big black-haired thunder cloud.

'You're packing,' he noted flatly.

Kat nodded uneasily, her mouth running dry as he stared in level challenge back at her.

'This is for you...' Mikhail tossed a jewellery box carelessly on the bed where it landed beside her suitcase. 'A small token of my...my appreciation,' he selected with cool precision.

Her heart beating very fast, Kat lifted the box and flipped it open to display a breathtaking emerald and diamond pendant. 'It's hardly small,' she told him, taken aback by the sheer size of the emerald and its deep glowing colour. 'What on earth do you expect me to do with this?'

'Wear it for me tonight. What you choose to do with it afterwards is entirely your business.'

'I suppose I ought to have said thank you straight away but I was rather overwhelmed by you giving me something so expensive,' she said apologetically.

An ebony brow rose. 'You expected something cheap and tacky to go with this ordinary kick you're suddenly on?'

'Of course not, but it's not a kick—*I'm* ordinary, Mikhail. And tomorrow I'm going back to my own life and it's ordinary as well,' Kat countered with quiet dignity as she set the jewellery box down on the dressing table and studied it with a sinking heart and a growing sense of desolation.

That spectacular emerald was his way of saying goodbye and thanks. She knew that so why was the fact that he was treating her exactly as she had expected him to treat her hurting her so much? Had she somehow thought that she might be different from her predecessors in his bed, that she might mean a little more to him? Pallor now spread below her fair complexion, her tummy succumbing to a nauseous lurch. Well, if she had thought that she was more special, she was being thoroughly punished for her vanity. He had just proved that she meant little more to him than a willing body on which he could ease his high-voltage sex drive. She had fulfilled his expectations and pleased him and now it was time for her to leave: it was that simple. She was no longer flavour of the month. She spun back to look at him, lounging in her doorway in an open-necked shirt and jeans, six feet five inches of unadulterated alpha male, absolutely gorgeous with his black hair ruffled by the breeze and a dark covering of stubble accentuating his handsome jaw line and wide expressive mouth. Tension screamed from him and she dropped her gaze, belatedly appreciating that he was not enjoying the process of putting her back out of his life any more than she was.

'I'll see you at dinner,' he told her and he walked away.

Hearts didn't break, Kat told herself as she clasped the pendant round her throat a couple of hours later. Hearts dented and bruised. She would head home tomorrow, sell the emerald to buy some security for her and her sisters and find a job. In truth, a new life awaited her, for the loss of the guest house was forcing her to strike out in an alternative direction. Where was her eagerness to greet that fresh start? She smoothed down the folds of the maxi dress, a colourful print that accentuated her bright hair and light skin. The emerald glowed at her throat, the surrounding diamonds twinkling to catch the light.

A knock sounded on the door. It was Lara, studying her with languid cool to say, 'Dinner is ready...I see you're packed and ready to go.'

Kat nodded. Lara had abandoned her friendly approaches once it became obvious that Kat and her boss had become lovers. 'Yes...'

'Are you upset?' Lara asked, disconcerting Kat once again.

Kat shrugged a bare shoulder as she concentrated on climbing the colourful glass staircase without tripping over her long skirt. 'Not really. Staying on *The Hawk* has been an experience but it's hardly been what I'm accustomed to. I'm looking forward to getting home, pulling on my jeans and gossiping with my sisters,' she fielded, pride lifting her head high, for she would have sooner thrown herself down the stairs than reveal just how cut up she truly was at the prospect of leaving Mikhail.

'The boss will be a hard act to follow. I hope you don't find that he's spoiled you for other men,' Lara commented.

'Who knows?' Kat quipped. Not for the first time it occurred to her that Mikhail's PA was a little too impressed by her boss and the unattainability factor he was famed for. The girl was gorgeous, Kat acknowledged, and perhaps it annoyed the beautiful blonde that Mikhail could remain impervious to her appeal while choosing to spend time with a woman who had neither Lara's glossy perfection nor her youth.

'The chef has really pushed the boat out tonight with the meal. Everyone knows you're leaving tomorrow,' Lara remarked laconically before she left her.

Lara had not been joking, Kat registered as her attention fell on the impressive dining table festooned in crisp pastel linen, sparkling candles and a light scattering of artistic pearls and rosebuds. Her brows rose as Mikhail strode out of the salon chatting on his cell phone in Russian. He put away the phone while studying her with shrewd assessing eyes. Was he looking for evidence of tears or sadness? Her chin tilted and a resolute smile softened Kat's tense lips as she took a seat.

'You look stunning this evening,' Mikhail said, startling her, for he rarely handed out compliments. 'The emerald brings out the remarkable green of your eyes, *milaya moya.*'

Bellini cocktails were brought to the table and then the meal was served and Kat's mortification began to climb, for the starter arrived cooked in a heart shape and every edible aphrodisiac known to man featured on the menu, accompanied by a good deal of chocolate. It was like an over-the-top Valentine's Day meal, wholly inappropriate for a couple on the brink of parting for ever. Mikhail, furthermore, preferred plain Russian food and a good deal of it, not the dainty elaborate portions he was being served.

'I suppose all this is in your honour,' he said drily, watching Kat bite into a chocolate truffle. 'Clearly my chef is your devoted slave.'

'Hardly that. François understands that I appreciate his efforts,' Kat countered lightly, for while Mikhail paid his staff well and rewarded them for excellence, he generally only spoke to them about their work when they did something to displease him, an attitude that Kat had combatted with praise and encouragement.

Sadly, on this particular occasion François' wonderful food was wasted on her because she was sitting there thinking that she would never dine with Mikhail again. He had treated her as he always did, with engrained good manners and light entertaining conversation. If he was ill at ease with the situation, it didn't show.

Kat, on the other hand, felt increasingly gutted by his steady self-control. She watched him, hungry for every last imprint of him, her troubled gaze winging constantly back to the remarkably beautiful eyes that illuminated his handsome face, the strength that dominated his features, and there was not a sign that he was experiencing an ounce of the regret that was torturing her. The remnants of the glorious truffle turned to ashes in her mouth. For a dangerous moment she wanted to cry and rail at the heavens for what Mikhail did not feel for her.

'I'm pretty tired tonight,' she admitted, although she already knew she would not enjoy a single wink of sleep.

'Go to bed. I'll join you later,' Mikhail breathed, his husky dark drawl smooth as a caress.

Halfway out of her chair, Kat froze, for it had not occurred to her that he might expect her to share his bed as usual. Had he no sensitivity, no comprehension of how she felt? Stifling her anger, she lifted her russet head. 'I hope you don't mind but I'd prefer to be on my own tonight.'

Mikhail frowned, for he had cherished a fantasy of seeing her reclining on his bed, those pale soft curves embellished only by the emerald he had bought her.

'It wouldn't feel right to be with you tonight,' Kat muttered in harried explanation, her pale face flushing with self-conscious colour. 'We're over and done now and I couldn't pretend otherwise.'

Mikhail was taken aback by that candid assessment and the insulting suggestion that she might have to *pretend* anything in his arms, and his stubborn mouth clenched hard. *Let it go*, logic dictated. A celibate night might not be what he wanted or even what he felt he deserved when he had handled her with kid gloves and all the respect he could muster, but even less was he in the mood for feminine drama. Not that Kat looked likely to offer him tears: her heart-shaped face was as still as a pond surface. With an odd little smile and a nod she walked away fast.

Dinner had felt like the condemned woman's last meal, Kat conceded wretchedly as she got ready for bed, but she wasn't going to cry about him. It was over and she would pick herself back up and go on. From the first moment they had met this hour of hurt and rejection had awaited her as surely as disillusionment. He said all the right things, he did all the right things, but he didn't *feel* them. There was only a superficial bond between them and it meant a lot less to him than it did to her. And so Kat tormented herself with wounding thoughts that kept her tossing and turning until she put the bedside light on at about two in the morning and dug out a magazine in the hope of quieting her overactive brain.

When a light knock sounded on the door that communicated with Mikhail's suite she froze as if a thunderclap had sounded and then slid out of bed in a rush. She had locked the door earlier, not because she feared he might ignore her desire to spend the night alone, but because she wanted to underline for her own benefit that their intimacy was now at an end. Now, with her heart beating very fast, she unlocked the door and opened it.

'I saw the light. You can't sleep either?' Mikhail had stepped back a couple of feet from the door, his lean, powerfully muscular body clad only in light boxer shorts.

'No, I can't.' Her palm sweated against the door, her heart thumping in her ear drums at an accelerated rate as she noted, really could not have avoided noticing, that he was sporting a hard-on that tented his boxers. Her mouth ran dry and she tore her gaze from him, heated colour burnishing her cheekbones.

'*Pridi ka mne*…come to me,' Mikhail murmured slightly raggedly, black eyes smouldering like fire-brands over her, lingering on the generous curve of her soft mouth.

And it was as if that one look lit a fire inside her treacherous body because her breasts stirred, the nip-ples tightening, and moist heat made her uncomfort-ably aware of the ache at the heart of her. She froze in denial of those lowering sensations. 'I *can't*,' she mut-tered tightly. 'It's over now. We're finished.'

Kat closed the door fast, shot the lock closed again and rested back against the cold unyielding wood to support her weak lower limbs. She had resisted him and she was proud of her self-discipline. Another bout of wildly exciting sex was not going to cure what ailed her heart and it would only make her feel ashamed of herself. It was one thing to love a man, another thing entirely to drop one's self-esteem in pursuit of him. Her teeth clenched, she moved back to the bed, doused the light and clambered below the sheet with hot tears stinging her eyes. She ignored the tears, determined not to let go of her control, determined not to greet him in the morning with swollen reddened eyes that would destroy her pride.

Cursing below his breath, Mikhail went for another cold shower. It was sex, that was all, he told himself. It was nothing to do with the fact that the bed felt empty without her and he missed her chatter. It was logical to end it, logical to guard against getting involved. When it came to a woman, he was far too clever and disciplined to give weight to illogical feelings and irrational and undoubtedly sexual promptings.

After a sleepless night, Kat asked for breakfast in her room, seeing no reason why she should put herself through another nerve-racking meeting with Mikhail. Indeed the less she saw of him before she left, the better, she told herself urgently. She dressed with great care in a smart blue shift dress and cardigan and used more make-up than usual to conceal the shadows below her eyes.

Lara phoned down to tell her that the helicopter that would take her to the airport for her flight was powering up. There was a note of satisfaction in the glamorous blonde's voice that even Kat could not have missed. Lara, without a doubt, was glad to see Kat leaving, Kat acknowledged ruefully, marvelling that she had for a while felt quite warm towards the young woman, for it was obvious to her now that Lara could never have honestly returned that friendliness. Had Lara been jealous of Kat's relationship with her boss? Was Lara in love with Mikhail?

Her cases having already been collected, Kat climbed the glass staircase for the very last time. She wouldn't miss the fancy stairs, she thought glumly. They were a colourfully confusing nightmare to use safely at night. From above her she could hear the calls of the crew as they made preparations for the helicopter to take off. As she emerged into the bright sunlight of a beautiful day Mikhail appeared, shocking her, for she had honestly believed that she would not see him again before she left. Sheathed in a lightweight designer beige suit teamed with a silk tie the colour of bronze, he looked incredibly handsome and incredibly assured. Certainly he bore no resemblance to a man who had endured a disturbed night, she conceded unhappily.

Mikhail stared at her, black diamond eyes narrowed and intense, a tiny muscle pulling taut at the corner of his unsmiling mouth. 'Kat…'

'Goodbye,' Kat told him briskly, baring her teeth in a resolute smile

'I don't want to say goodbye…' The words might have been physically wrenched from Mikhail because he clamped his handsome mouth shut again as if an involuntary admission had been dragged from him.

'But we must,' Kat countered with quiet dignity, nodding an acknowledgement at Stas, who was stationed tensely by the rail about ten feet away.

'You're wrong…there is no *must*.'

Kat blinked and frowned and focused her attention on the helicopter and all the fuss taking place around it that suggested that the craft was ready for an imminent departure.

'*Stay*…' Mikhail ground out with staggering abruptness.

Her head swivelled back to him, green eyes wide with disbelief. 'What on earth are you saying?'

His face was taut with self-discipline. 'I want you to stay with me.'

'But it's all organised that I'm leaving… *You* organised it, for goodness' sake!' she reminded him in angry bewilderment.

The pilot came to a halt six feet away and informed Mikhail that the helicopter was good to go.

Mikhail ignored him, but as Kat took a step in the pilot's direction a hand like an iron vice closed round her forearm to prevent her. *'Stay!'* he ground out again between visibly clenched even white teeth.

'I can't!' Kat gasped strickenly, baffled by his behaviour and appalled to feel a giant wash of tears welling up at the backs of her eyes as if all the stress, all the unhappiness she had undergone over the previous twenty-four hours was finally set to overflow.

Mikhail closed his free hand over her other forearm, holding her captive in front of him. Thickly lashed black eyes clashed with hers and there was an urgency there that she had never seen before. 'I need you to stay,' he muttered hoarsely. 'I need you to stay because I *can't* let you go.'

And that plea moved her and made her listen and look as nothing else could have done. For the space of an impossibly stressful minute she had thought she was dealing with a male whim voiced on impulse and most probably motivated by sexual desire. But, *'I need you,'* from a male as incredibly self-sufficient and reserved as Mikhail carried serious weight with her. 'You're hurting my arms,' she framed shakily, because his grip was too tight.

He gave a muffled curse as his long brown fingers sprang open to free her, and he shot something in Russian at Stas before bending to scoop Kat up into his strong arms and stride back indoors with her again.

'This can't be happening—this isn't right!' Kat protested vehemently.

'It is the first right thing I have done this week,' Mikhail informed her with immoveable conviction as he carted her into the salon and out to the private deck, where he sank down on a sofa with her still clasped firmly in his arms. 'You are staying with me, *moyo zolotse—*'

Kat was thoroughly bemused by his forceful behaviour. 'But you *can't* simply change your mind like that at the last minute.'

Shrewd black eyes gazed down in challenge at her. 'If I recognise a wrong decision, should I not put it right? Kat—have you any idea how rarely I admit to being in the wrong?'

Kat had an excellent idea, but he had plunged her into turmoil. She had hyped herself up to leave him and it had taken every ounce of her strength to retain her composure in the face of that challenge. His sudden change of heart, however, had steamrollered over her defensive barriers as nothing else could have done. 'I can't just stay with you,' she said again, her voice shaky and lacking its usual energy. 'I've got a life and a family to get back to, Mikhail.'

Her lips parted again. 'You were finished with me. It was over…that's what you wanted— '

'If it was genuinely over, I'd have let you leave. Keeping you was a gut instinct,' Mikhail confessed harshly.

A gut instinct? Where did that leave her? One minute he was getting rid of her, the next he was snatching her back from the brink. 'But what happens now?' she whispered unsteadily, suddenly cold and shivering even in the protective circle of his arms.

His powerful chest expanded as he breathed in deep. 'I take you home with me.'

Her brows climbed. 'You take me *home* with you? Am I a pet all of a sudden?'

'I'm asking you to move in with me. I've never asked a woman to do that before,' Mikhail revealed quietly.

Kat examined the idea, taken aback by it and then alarmed by how much she liked the images springing to mind. But it was a commitment, far more of a commitment than acting as a man's companion and lover on board a yacht for a month. Yes, it was definitely a commitment, she registered dizzily, and suddenly her eyes were overflowing with the tears she had held back with such tenacity.

'What's wrong?' Mikhail demanded, a long forefinger skimming the glistening trail of moisture marking her cheek.

'Nothing! I'm just leaking!' Kat gasped defensively, dashing the tears away with an impatient hand. 'But I *can't* just move in with you. I have commitments too—'

'Your sisters? I will look after them as if they were my own flesh and blood,' Mikhail told her with a sudden expansive smile.

'But I've to sort out the farmhouse, make arrangements—'

'You will leave all such responsibilities to me. You will move in with me, take care of me and my home and that is *all* you need to worry about in the future. Is that understood?'

Kat closed her eyes tight because the tears were still welling up and she was biting back a sob and loving and hating him simultaneously: loving him for recognising that they had found something special, hating him for springing it on her in such a last minute way that she couldn't be fully convinced by it. 'What if you change your mind again?' she asked in a wobbly undertone. 'What if this isn't what you want in a few weeks' time?'

'That's a risk I'm prepared to take. I will always be honest with you and I don't want to lose you.'

Kat swallowed back the thickness in her throat and struggled to breathe at a regular rate again. She supposed she couldn't expect him to say much more, for they would both be on the same learning curve together.

He didn't want to lose her yet he had very nearly let her go. How very close he had come to doing that would probably always haunt her. If she had left on that helicopter, would he have come after her?

'I own a country house that I believe you will like,' Mikhail volunteered. 'You can invite your sisters there, treat it as though it was your own home and next week you can attend Luka's wedding with me as my partner.'

Her restive fingers clenched on the edge of his silk-and-linen-mix jacket, wet clogged eye lashes lifting on drenched green eyes as she stared up into his handsome face, her heart pounding like a piston engine.

His forefinger gently traced the generous curve of her lower lip. 'It will work beautifully…you'll see,' Mikhail forecast with his usual invincible confidence, and then he kissed her with passionate urgency and thought took a hike from her head.

At the end of that day she lay in his bed, her body weak and sated from the hungry demands of his, and she wondered if she had been foolish to agree to stay with him. Was she merely putting off the heartbreak that awaited her? Extending her suffering? She loved him like crazy, but was very much afraid that he was simply in lust with her and not yet ready to give that pleasure up.

CHAPTER TEN

MIKHAIL LISTENED TO the lawyer's advice only because he paid generously for all advice that offered him greater financial protection. But he was immoveable when it came to the issue of presenting Kat with another legal agreement, on this occasion one relating to her status as his live-in lover. No way was he making that mistake again! He had still to hear the last from her lips regarding the previous agreement, and in any case he was convinced that Kat didn't have a mercenary bone in her body. Time and time again she had spurned the chance to enrich herself at his expense. Even though she had been desperate for money to settle her debts when they first met, her bill for that one night of accommodation in her former home had been ridiculously modest.

'My girlfriend is not a gold-digger,' Mikhail murmured levelly. 'I am not that much of a fool. I can scent a gold-digger at a hundred yards.'

'Situations change, *people* change,' the smooth-talking legal eagle pointed out speciously. 'It is of crucial importance that you consider the future and protect yourself.'

Mikhail reckoned that he had been protecting himself all his life in one way or another, so there was nothing new in that idea. Protecting himself was second nature. He was well aware that he was still feeling punch drunk at the roaring success of letting Kat into his life on a less temporary basis. That had proved to be an excellent move and he was certainly reaping the benefits on the home front. If it was possible to bottle the essence of Kat, he would be constantly drunk. An abstracted smile curled his handsome mouth as he thought of Kat in his hot tub, Kat in his bed, Kat at his dining table, Kat...whenever and wherever he wanted her. After a mere six weeks he was happy to judge his new living arrangements as the essence of perfection. Even better, he had worked out exactly where his father had gone wrong in his relationships with women. The true secret was moderation. He didn't allow himself the pleasure of Kat *every* night; he carefully rationed himself to ensure that she did not become too necessary to his comfort. Sometimes he stayed over quite deliberately in the city and pleaded the pressure of work. Sometimes he didn't phone her, although she was getting remarkably good at phoning him to ask why he hadn't phoned, which rather put paid to the point of that attempt to set out his boundaries. As long as he stayed in control, however, he foresaw no problems.

'Are you considering marriage?' the lawyer asked in a bald enquiry.

Mikhail frowned and compressed his lips at the question.

'Do you think your Russian is considering marrying you?' Emmie was asking her sister at that exact same moment as she zipped up the frock Kat was trying on in the spacious cubicle. 'You know...is the living with him a trial for the ultimate commitment in his eyes?'

'No. Mikhail seems quite happy with where we are now,' Kat pronounced thoughtfully. 'He's very cautious… What do you think of this dress?'

'The silver metallic one has the most impact. I already told you that,' Emmie repeated, smoothing an abstracted hand over the obvious swell of her own pregnant stomach as she too looked in the mirror at their combined reflection. 'I just don't want you to be hurt, Kat…and goodness knows, you're not getting any younger—'

'Like I need that reminder!' Kat quipped with a wry laugh.

'Yes, but it is something you need to seriously consider. If you do want children some day you haven't got much time left to play with.'

'Emmie, only a few months ago there was no man in my life,' Kat reminded her ruefully. 'I certainly can't expect the first one who comes along in years to want to start a family with me. That would be a big ask for a guy who shies away from serious commitment.'

'Have you discussed the subject with him?' Emmie asked.

Kat stiffened, her thoughts hurtling back several weeks to the evening she had received the proof that their contraceptive oversight on the yacht had not resulted in conception. Mikhail had absorbed the news without comment, revealing neither relief nor regret, but Kat had been shocked by the stark wave of disappointment that had consumed her. As she had spent so many years raising her siblings she had always assumed that she would never crave the added responsibility of having a child of her own. Unfortunately for her, somehow even being with Mikhail had given her a powerful yearning for a baby, but she was utterly convinced that nothing would ever come of it.

Mikhail had brought her into his life but he wasn't building his life around her, Kat reflected sadly. He had moved her into Danegold Hall, his impossibly impressive Georgian country house, and urged her to make whatever changes she thought necessary there, only that was not an invitation to take too much to heart when the male giving it really didn't give a damn about his surroundings as long as he was comfortable. He had made the move easy for her by sending professional packers to Birkside. Her belongings and the pieces of furniture that Emmie didn't want were now stored in a barn on the estate for her to go through at her leisure. Emmie was living in the farmhouse now, drawing up plans to open a business while earning a living from the pedestrian job she had found locally. But on her days off, Emmie regularly got on the train and met up with her sister in London for a shopping trip. On this particular occasion the sisters were looking for a dress for Kat to wear to Luka Volkov's wedding.

'Kat?' Emmie persisted.

'Look, Mikhail's only thirty. He's got years and years ahead of him when he can choose to have a family and naturally he's not in any hurry,' Kat said lightly.

'But if he loves you—'

'I don't think he loves me. I don't think I'm in a for-ever-and-ever relationship with him,' Kat confided truthfully, lifting the silver dress off the hook and heading gratefully off to pay for it with one of the string of credit cards that Mikhail had insisted she accepted from him.

Even so, Kat disliked feeling like a kept woman and she would have preferred to look for employment. But

Mikhail wanted her to be available when he was free and able to travel if need be and there was no way she would be able to manage that feat and him and his vast Georgian home and even larger staff there if she had a job to go to every day. She had had to ask herself which was more important: her pride and independence or her love. And love had won because when Kat wasn't being tormented by her various sisters' awkward questions about her relationship with Mikhail, she was deliriously happy, certainly much happier than she had ever thought she could be. He was the sun, the moon and the stars for her, but she knew that she had to accept that outside the bounds of marriage many such relationships eventually came to an end.

Her phone buzzed. It was Mikhail.

'Meet me at the office and we'll go for lunch, *milaya moya,*' he suggested huskily, his dark deep drawl sending a responsive tremor down her spine.

Kat smiled into the phone, delighted that he was so eager to see her. He had stayed in his city apartment the night before and she had missed him. Possibly he had missed her as well, she reasoned with satisfaction, for otherwise he would have been willing to wait until he got back to the hall later that evening to see her.

Emmie gave her a stern look. 'He owns you…that's what I don't like.'

Kat's eyes widened in dismay. 'What on earth do you mean?'

'You're like…*addicted* to him,' Emmie pronounced with unhidden distaste and disapproval. 'Even Topsy noticed that weekend she stayed with you that when Mikhail enters the room, you can't see anyone else but him.'

'I do love him and I don't think it does Topsy any

harm to see that I care deeply for the man I'm living with,' Kat said gently, wishing she knew more about the background to Emmie's pregnancy, for with every week that passed Emmie seemed to be becoming more of a man hater.

A limo whisked Kat to Mikhail's London headquarters. She was accompanied by Ark, Stas' kid brother. Mikhail, from Kat's point of view, appeared to be obsessed by the idea that she might be mugged or attacked and had insisted she accepted Ark's presence when she was out in public. Only when she had recognised that that risk was a source of very genuine concern for him had she finally agreed, but she often felt sorry for Ark, reduced to hanging around bored while she shopped or sat gossiping over lengthy coffee sessions with her sisters.

Mikhail was in a meeting when Kat arrived and she stowed her shopping by the wall and sat down in Lara's office to wait while Ark hovered in the corridor.

Lara glided across the room to greet her with a rather tight smile of welcome and bent down to study more closely the emerald pendant that Kat wore. 'May I see it?' the other woman prompted politely.

Kat flushed with self-consciousness and nodded uneasy agreement as Lara minutely examined the emerald. She guessed that the other woman probably thought the pendant was far too ostentatious to wear out on a shopping trip and Kat could actually have agreed with her on that score. But the sticking point was how Mikhail felt about it. Mikhail *loved* to see Kat with the emerald round her neck and Kat wore it frequently to please him.

'The jewel is magnificent,' the gorgeous blonde commented thinly, overpowering envy souring her flawless features as she stepped back from her examination.

'The word is that the boss has never spent so much on a gift for a woman—you must feel very pleased with yourself.'

Kat's fine brows pleated in surprise and she flung the blonde a startled glance, not quite sure if Lara could have meant that comment the way it had sounded. 'No, that's not how I feel. I'm just…happy,' she breathed in a discomfited tone, offended at the suspicion that Lara could suspect that she might only be with Mikhail for his wealth.

'Of course you're happy. Why would you not be? *Suka!*' Lara snapped sharply, at which point, unnoticed by either woman, Ark put his head round the door to peer into the room. 'But I could tell you something that would wipe that smug smile right off your face!'

No longer suffering the misapprehension that her understanding was at fault, Kat gave the younger woman a cool appraisal. 'I don't think that's a good idea, Lara.'

'Well, I will tell you whether you want to know or not!' Lara practically spat the words at her. 'Remember that night before you were supposed to leave the yacht? Mikhail spent that night with me…that's how little you matter to him!'

The blood drained from Kat's face. Suddenly her skin felt clammy and the palms she had pressed to the handbag on her lap felt damp. For a moment she could not even make sense of what the other woman was saying and only knew that she was being verbally attacked. Just as quickly she was recalling that night that she had spent alone and sleepless and she was also recalling Mikhail's knock on her door. Her tummy lurched in stricken protest.

'Didn't you realise that he slept with me as well?' Lara queried, lifting a scornful brow at such apparent stupidity. 'He always has. I don't make demands on him. I'm *always* available...'

Out of nowhere the strength returned to Kat's rigid body and she leapt upright. She dragged her shattered gaze from the furious blonde and walked out of the door, ignoring the lift and Ark's query to head for the stairs instead. She needed some time on her own to think about the bombshell Lara had delivered and what she would have to do about it. She fled down the fire stairs, flight after flight, heard Ark shout after her and kept on going, not wanting anyone to see or speak to her in the state she was in. Her hurrying feet took her straight out of the building and into the welcome and anonymous crush of the lunchtime crowds on the pavement.

Her heart thudding so fast she was convinced she could hear it actually thumping in her ears, Kat walked at a smart pace with no destination in view. Only the fact that her high-heeled shoes had not been made for that amount of walking finally pierced her miasma of misery. Wincing at the sharp pinches of pain assailing her feet, Kat then headed into a café to get a seat. There she sat hunched over a cup of tea, as dazed as if her head had been struck in an accident. At that point she heard her phone ringing and she pulled it out, saw she had received about six missed calls from Mikhail and switched it off because she didn't want to speak to him, didn't *have* to speak to him, she consoled herself. She sat there a long time struggling to get the turmoil of her thoughts into some kind of rational order.

Lara was an absolutely gorgeous-looking young woman, very glossy and sophisticated and exactly the sort of woman whom Kat had often secretly believed Mikhail *should* have chosen as a girlfriend in place of

herself. Why would Lara tell such a lie? In fact, like it
or not, the evidence suggested that Lara was telling the
truth. Why? For the simple reason that Lara must have
been with Mikhail that night to be so certain that he had
not been with Kat. Every other night Kat and Mikhail
had shared his suite but that one night, which Lara had
chosen to mention, Kat had slept alone. Mikhail had
had motive and opportunity. Had he taken advantage
of it? Had he been carrying on a casual long-term affair
with his PA even before he met Kat? She shuddered at
the suspicion, sick with pain, jealousy and a growing
sense of despair. How could she have been so wrong
about the man she loved?

Back at his office in the wake of the drama Kat's sudden exit had caused, Mikhail was also thinking about
bad choices and his expression was as hard as granite.
In a crisis he was discovering that his strict policy of
moderation in his relationship with Kat had a serious
basic design flaw. Moderation had kicked him in the
teeth when he least expected it: she wouldn't even take
a phone call from him. And now she was gone, *lost*,
upset, maybe even upset enough to walk out in front of
a bus or something stupid like that, he thought with a
fear that had a ferociously aggressive edge unfamiliar
to his usual self-discipline.

Over her cooling tea, Kat realised that whatever she
chose to do she had no choice other than to return first
to Danegold Hall. Her passport, important documents,
everything she couldn't simply get by without was there.
Feeling cold inside and out and fighting distress, Kat
headed for the railway station. She might prefer to avoid
Mikhail but she had to be practical as well and walking
out on her life with him without forethought and planning wasn't possible. In any case, if he had any sense at

all, he would be equally keen to avoid the fallout from Lara's revelation—that was assuming Lara admitted what she had done. Ark had heard some of that conversation though, Kat reckoned in mortification, and no doubt Ark would tell his brother, Stas, who would tell Mikhail what they thought he needed to know.

On the train journey, Kat saw nothing of the passing scenery for a constant parade of mental images was playing through her head. Her brain was scouring every glimpse she had ever had of Lara and Mikhail together in the same room in search of some proof of Lara's claim. What amazed Kat then was the reality that she had often been baffled by the way Mikhail treated Lara like a piece of office equipment, seemingly impervious to his PA's stunning beauty and appeal. Kat had not once witnessed the smallest sign of awareness or intimacy between them. Indeed on the face of it Mikhail and Lara hadn't even seemed that friendly. Their working relationship was distant and formal, untouched by banter or even a hint of flirtation.

Could Mikhail be that smooth and effective at deception? That he could treat a lover as though she were nothing more than a barely regarded employee? Kat frowned, for in her experience Mikhail was more naturally blunt and open in nature, so that she could quite easily tell when something annoyed or irritated or worried him. But then, to be fair, he himself had remarked that she was unusually accurate in her ability to read his thoughts. She had almost told him that that was because she loved him and when it came to him love seemed to have given her keener powers of observation. That was how she knew that when he lifted a brow in a certain way he was irritated, that when he moved his hands or stilled them altogether he was usually angry, and that when his mouth compressed it was usually a sign of concern.

On the other hand, men didn't automatically regard the kind of casual sex that Lara had suggested had taken place over a sustained period as a tie worthy of acknowledgement. In that way, sex could be treated as being of no more account than a meal. Was that how Mikhail might have rationalised such behaviour? Had he been amusing himself with Lara on the sidelines while Kat agonised about whether or not she would sleep with him? It was a humiliating, wounding suspicion. Until that moment it had not occurred to her how much she had valued Mikhail's apparent willingness to wait for her to share his bed or her natural assumption that no other woman was satisfying his needs while Kat remained unavailable.

When she got off the train Kat assumed she would have to phone for a taxi and wait because she had not informed anyone what time she was arriving, but she was greeted on the platform by one of Mikhail's drivers and she slid into the waiting Bentley with a sinking heart. Had *he* already guessed that she would soon be back at Danegold Hall? Was she now honour-bound to stage some ghastly sordid confrontation over the head of Lara? Of course, if he was there and she was moving out she would have to give him some sort of explanation. She comforted herself with the awareness that Mikhail would only be home during the day mid-week on the very rarest of occasions and wondered if a brief note would do, in which she would say something meaningless but not unpleasant such as that things were not working out for her.

She ought to hate him, she thought painfully, wondering what the matter with her was. Perhaps she was still too much in shock to be thinking clearly, she reckoned wretchedly, in shock that Mikhail was not the man she had honestly believed he was and that he was a much more lightweight, untrustworthy and dishonest individual than she could ever have guessed from the way he had treated her. Ironically he had treated her very well. So, did he think that sexual infidelity was unimportant? She remembered the clusters of eager young woman who had surrounded him every time he went out in public and accepted that temptation must often have come his way. Yet to have slept with a woman who worked for him, whom Kat knew and accepted, was beyond forgiveness.

Kat mounted the steps to the front door, which was already standing open with Reeves, Mikhail's imperturbable butler, stationed there. With a pained smile in response to his greeting, Kat limped in, acknowledging that if anything her feet were hurting her even more than they had earlier that afternoon. Maybe taking them off on the train had been unwise. Halfway across the hall she came to a halt, slid the beautiful but too-tight shoes off and walked barefoot up the stairs. She headed straight to the bedroom she shared with Mikhail and the dressing room where a miniature trunk held everything from her passport to her birth certificate. She lifted out the papers, slapped them down on the bed and went off to locate a suitcase. She couldn't believe she was leaving the man she loved, couldn't bear even the thought of it, yet knew she had no choice. Lara could only have known that Mikhail had not slept with Kat that night if Lara had spent that same night with him: her brain could not get past that fact.

From drawers she dug out a few basic changes of clothing. She wasn't fool enough to try and pack everything. She would just take what was necessary for a couple of weeks and ask for the rest to be sent on to her. She supposed she would move back to the farmhouse with Emmie and knew her sibling would be glad to have company. What price her fine sensitivity about accepting the house from Mikhail now?

'You're not even giving me a chance to defend myself?'

Kat froze and spun to see Mikhail poised in the doorway, his lean darkly handsome face grim and taut as he asked that question. He had discarded his tie and his jacket and stood there in shirt sleeves, his black diamond eyes hard. He was toughing Lara's confession out, Kat assumed, determined to admit no fault. She turned her head away from him because she felt as if her heart were breaking inside her.

'Kat?' Mikhail prompted.

'Yes, I heard what you said but I don't really know how to respond. Sometimes it's best to say nothing. I don't want to argue with you—what's the point?'

'The point is *us,*' Mikhail growled. 'Isn't what we have worth fighting for?'

Kat dropped the clothing in her hands into the open case and shot him a furious glance of reproach. 'OK. Did you sleep with her?'

'No,' Mikhail framed succinctly, hard dark eyes challenging her.

Kat turned back to her packing. 'Well, of course you're going to say *that,*' she told him, totally unimpressed.

'What the hell was the point of asking me, then?' Mikhail roared back at her. 'You know you've put me through one hell of an afternoon?'

Refusing to be intimidated by that lion's roar, Kat

kept on packing. 'I can't say that I enjoyed my afternoon either—'

'First of all I had to put up with a melodramatic tantrum from an employee, then you went *missing*!' He stressed the word.

Infuriated, Kat whipped back to him. 'I did not go missing!'

'How do you think I felt when you took off after that nonsense Lara spouted to you? I was worried sick about you!' Mikhail bit out furiously. 'I knew you were upset and—'

Kat lifted a russet brow and turned to him again, hating him at that minute, convinced she knew exactly why he was behaving the way he was. 'How could you *know* I was upset? You got a spy hotline to my brain or something? I wasn't upset. Naturally I was surprised, rather disgusted, in fact,' she confided with growing vigour. 'And I needed some time to myself—'

'You needed time to yourself to think about that poison like you needed a hole in the head!' Mikhail shot back at her with lethal derision.

'Don't you *dare* shout at me!' Kat shrieked back at him.

Sudden smouldering silence fell. Mikhail breathed in deep and slow, his broad chest expanding. 'I didn't intend to shout.'

'When you've been accused of infidelity, bellowing like a bull in a china shop is not a good idea,' Kat informed him curtly.

'*Wrongly* accused,' Mikhail fired back at her, his stunning dark eyes scorching hot with annoyance. 'That is the crucial fact.'

'Mikhail…' Kat swallowed hard and collected her churning thoughts, unhappiness bowing her shoulders like a giant weight as she accepted that the scene could not be avoided. 'Lara knew that we didn't spend that last night together before I was supposed to leave *The Hawk*. She must've been with you that night to know that.'

'Wrong!' Mikhail framed grittily. 'She was standing on the deck outside the office below us eavesdropping on our last exchange over dinner that night when you told me you wanted to sleep alone. So, if that's your only piece of evidence against me, you're on a losing streak!'

Kat's lashes fluttered in confusion. 'Are you sure that's how she knew we were sleeping apart?'

'How the hell else could she have known?' Mikhail swore suddenly in Russian and shifted his hands as he moved towards her. 'Kat, you saw me at three in the morning that same night and I was still in my own room,' he reminded her.

'Yes, but—'

Mikhail withdrew a mobile phone from his pocket and pressed several buttons. 'Watch this…' he urged. 'Stas was clever enough to record Lara screaming at me…'

Kat focused on the screen and saw a flurry of blurred movement and heard a noise. The blur became Lara, blonde hair whipping round her enraged face and she was shouting. 'Why didn't you want me? You could have had me! What's wrong with you that you didn't want me? She's old, she's past it! It's an insult. I'm young and beautiful—how could she be the one you move into your home?'

Kat was transfixed. There were another few sentences of distraught ranting from Lara before she suddenly appreciated that a camera was recording her tantrum and she launched herself at Stas in a vitriolic fury, whereupon the recording came to a sudden telling halt.

Mikhail switched it off. 'Do you want to see it again?' he enquired smoothly.

'No…' Kat's admission was small, her face heavily flushed with chagrin. She had listened to a vain and immature hysteric's fantasy and swallowed her ridiculous lies as solid fact. Her legs were wobbly and she sank down on the edge of the bed with *'old, past it!'* still ringing unpleasantly in her ears.

'Ark heard everything she said to you, his attention drawn by the fact that she called you a rude word in Russian,' Mikhail explained. 'He informed me and I confronted her and, as you saw, she went crazy. There was a lot more that Stas didn't manage to record. She was jealous of you and furious that I didn't find her attractive but the situation that developed today was still my fault.'

'How was it your fault?' Kat asked limply, shot from the conviction that he was an unfaithful rat to the conviction that she had misjudged him at such speed that her head was still spinning. She felt dizzy and bewildered and stupid, much as though a huge rock had landed on her from a height.

'Lara came on to me when I first hired her. That's happened to me many times and I didn't consider it sufficient grounds to sack her.'

Kat's eyes were wide with consternation at the news. 'You…*didn't?*'

'I made it clear I wasn't interested and as a rule that is sufficient to bring an end to such behaviour, but Lara is extremely vain about her own attractions and her resentment grew when you came into my life. I suspect she tried to cause trouble between us before in small ways. Luckily she wasn't close enough to me to have the power to do more. I think you can probably blame her for the horrible make-up you wore the first night when you dined with me.'

'And for not telling me when to meet you,' Kat guessed.

'And persuading you to wear red that evening at the club—I hate the colour red, always have,' he confided.

'Such trivial things,' Kat commented seriously. 'I'm grateful she didn't have the ability to cause more trouble.'

'Lara isn't clever enough to appreciate that a man wants a woman for more than her looks…'

Kat wasn't quite sure how to take that statement.

Mikhail laughed out loud, his amusement smashing the strained silence. He snatched up her case and tossed it on the floor and sank down beside her on the bed. 'I find you much more beautiful than Lara.'

'You couldn't possibly. I'm old and past it,' Kat muttered shakily, the tears gathering.

'You knocked me sideways the very first time I saw you. And you had class and strength and you refused to want me back, which shocked me.'

'It did you good to have a woman say no to you for a change,' Kat countered a shade tartly, unwilling to let all her tension go for fear that something bad was still about to happen that would part them.

Mikhail curved a powerful arm round her taut body to draw her close. 'It did, but the fear of losing you that I suffered today almost brought me to my knees,' he admitted gruffly. 'I was so determined to stay in control of our relationship and not give way to my strong feelings for you, and then suddenly I was facing the prospect of losing you and all that seemed so trivial in comparison—'

'Strong feelings?' Kat prompted, one small hand awkwardly engaged in stroking the arm wound round her.

His fingers curved to her chin to turn her face gently round to his. His eyes were warmer than she had ever seen them. 'I love you very much, Kat…so much I can't contemplate a life without you. But until today I saw that as a weakness and a fault. I watched my father slowly drink himself to death after he lost my mother. He was cruel to her and he was never faithful, but when she died he went to pieces. He was much more dependent on her than any of us ever realised,' he related ruefully. 'I was terrified of ever needing a woman that much. I thought he was an obsessional personality. I thought I had to protect myself from that because, in common with my father, I do tend to be rather intense in personality, and then I met you and right from the start you had a very potent effect on me…'

The chill still inside Kat was soothed by the tenderness in his gaze and his honesty and she pushed her face into a broad muscular shoulder, revelling in the warm familiar scent of him and the new sense of soul-deep security flooding her. 'I love you too,' she whispered fervently.

'You should have guessed how I felt about you that morning I prevented you from boarding the helicopter,' Mikhail muttered with a frown. 'I tried to make myself let you go and I found that I literally *couldn't* face sending you away. The night before was the longest and worst night of my life. I wanted you. I needed you: choice didn't come into it. You've owned my heart ever since.'

'That may be so, but you've been pretty good at hiding it,' Kat voiced, although when she thought back to recent weeks it occurred to her that he had probably shown it every time he looked at her, every time he curled her into his arms and held her tight through the night, only unfortunately she had been too insecure to recognise and interpret what she was seeing.

'I won't be hiding it any more. If you had known I loved you today you might have been more inclined to talk to me and trust my word rather than Lara's. Would you have believed me without having seen that recording?'

'Yes…deep down inside me it was a real struggle to believe that you would behave that way,' Kat acknowledged with quiet certainty.

Mikhail lifted her hand and carefully threaded a ring onto her wedding finger. 'I've had this in my possession since the first day you moved in.'

Kat studied the fabulous diamond solitaire with wide eyes of sheer wonderment. 'But you resisted giving it to me?'

'Yes. I'm a stubborn man, *lubov moya,*' Mikhail groaned. 'That means, "my love" and you are the only woman I've ever loved. You've had the chance to see the worst of me. Will you still marry me? And soon?'

'Oh, absolutely,' Kat carolled, flattening him to the mattress in a sudden marked demonstration of enthusiasm. 'As soon as it can be arranged…when I let you out of bed, which is not going to be any time soon,' she warned him with sparkling eyes from which the last shadow of insecurity had fled.

A wolfish grin of satisfaction slashed his handsome mouth. 'I should have given you the ring the day I bought it.'

'Yes, you're a slow learner as well as stubborn,' his future wife conceded. 'But you did buy the ring weeks ago, which gains you points...not that you need them.'

'I only need you,' Mikhail told her, running his fingers lazily through the spirals of her russet hair. 'And I won't feel secure until I see my wedding ring on your hand.'

His phone buzzed.

'Switch it off,' she said.

A hint of consternation entered his beautiful eyes. 'Have I created a monster?' he murmured with flaring amusement.

Kat ran a rousing hand quite deliberately along a muscular male thigh and he tensed with sensual anticipation. 'I'll switch it off,' he promised instantly. 'Sometimes I'm a very fast learner, *dusha moya*.'

And so was Kat, bending over him to kiss him with a confidence she had never had before while trying to keep a lid on the wild, surging happiness assailing her in glorious waves. He was hers, finally, absolutely hers, her dream come true, and some day he would accept that being obsessionally in love with a woman who loved him every bit as intensely could be wonderful, rather than threatening.

EPILOGUE

THREE YEARS LATER, Kat stood at the foot of the pair of cots in the nursery at Danegold Hall, proudly surveying her twins, Petyr and Olga. They were both tiny and dark-haired with their newborn eyes of blue slowly turning green. Her son, Petyr, was lively, restless and slept very little while Olga was altogether a much more laid-back baby.

As far as their mother was concerned the twins were her personal miracle and, even two months after their birth, she could still hardly believe they were her children. After all, after she and Mikhail had married she hadn't fallen pregnant as she had hoped. It hadn't happened and eventually after fertility tests that proved nothing conclusive she had gone for IVF treatment in a top Russian clinic. She had found the process stressful and hard on the nerves, and the first time they had been very disappointed when conception failed to take place, but the second time she had undergone the process she had conceived. It would have been hard for her to describe the boundless joy she had experienced when she saw the two tiny shapes in her womb on a scan some weeks later. She hadn't even realised that tears were running down her cheeks until Mikhail turned her round to dry her face for her.

The twins' birth had been straightforward, a relief for Mikhail, who had barely let her out of his sight for longer than twelve hours during her entire pregnancy. What had happened to his own mother when she tried to deliver his sibling had still haunted him and had given him the impression that giving birth was the most dangerous thing even a healthy woman could choose to do. Only then had she truly understood why Mikhail had been so careful to tell her that he could be content with her even if they never had children. At the time she had been hurt, worried that he didn't really want a child, but she had been utterly wrong in that fear. Mikhail had been terrified that something might go wrong and had had so many top doctors standing around when she delivered the twins that she ought to have been delivering sextuplets at the very least. Her eyes still stung when she recalled Mikhail pulling her into his arms afterwards, barely acknowledging the existence of his newborn twins to whisper shakily, 'Thank God you are safe. That is all that has concerned me this day, *lyubov' moya.*'

Even after three years, her husband loved her every bit as much as she loved him. Indeed the depth of the bond between them had gone from strength to strength since they married. Once that was achieved, Mikhail's sense of security had enabled him to drop what remained of his reserve. And, as he had promised, he had embraced her sisters as though they were his own so that she was as close to her siblings as she had ever been.

'Gloating again...?' a familiar accented drawl teased.

'Sorry, can't help it, still can't believe they're ours,' Kat confided, her bright head turning to focus on the darkly handsome male poised in the doorway, a flock of butterflies taking flight inside her tummy. Mikhail's effect on her hormones never faded, she thought, her face warming. And how could it have done? He was drop-dead gorgeous.

A faint smile curving his sensual lips, her husband joined her to stare down at their son and daughter. 'They do look cute when they're not squalling,' he conceded with amusement. 'This morning they looked like little red-faced dictators when they woke up.'

'They were hungry,' their mother proclaimed defensively.

Mikhail turned her slowly round. 'So am I, *laskovaya moya*. I am very hungry to have my beautiful wife all to myself for a few days.'

Her sparkling green eyes rounded as she leant up against his lean, powerful body, one hand resting on a broad shoulder. 'Have you actually taken some time off?'

'Even better. I've arranged a holiday for us on a deserted island.'

'Doesn't sound the kind of place you can take babies.'

'They're not coming.' Lean, strong face resolute, Mikhail gazed down at his wife as she parted her generous mouth to object. 'Your sisters are going to look after them for us. Our third wedding anniversary is an important occasion and I want to do something special.'

'But, we *can't* leave them behind—'

A black brow quirked. 'Even with two nannies and your sisters and the entire household staff to look after them?'

Kat's even white teeth worried at her full lower lip in indecision.

'I need you too,' Mikhail husked, lowering his dark head to caress her mouth slowly with his in exactly the way she could never resist, leaving her breathless and quivering. 'And I think you need me in the same way.'

'Well…' Kat hesitated. 'A deserted island?'

'White beach, blue sea, no clothes,' Mikhail outlined.

'So that's the fantasy?' Kat laughed, loving his honesty as much as she loved him and the surprise break he had organised.

'The fantasy I have every intention of turning into fact,' her husband countered with a lethally sexy look in his black diamond eyes. 'More pleasure than you can believe…'

'Oh, I can believe,' she confirmed dizzily, breathless at the smouldering look of desire in his stunning gaze. 'You always deliver.'

'I'm crazy about you,' Mikhail muttered thickly, claiming her mouth in a passionate kiss that sent her every sense singing.

Kat was too happy and too bound up in that kiss to reply. A second honeymoon on a deserted island, Mikhail all to herself. No, she had not a single complaint about that plan of action.

* * * * *

COMING NEXT MONTH from Harlequin Presents®
AVAILABLE MAY 21, 2013

#3145 THE SHEIKH'S PRIZE
A Bride for a Billionaire
Lynne Graham
Marrying Sapphire Marshall was the biggest mistake of Sheikh Zahir's life. Now, his ex-wife has returned to his desert and Zahir plans to banish her from his mind once and for all, beginning with reclaiming his wedding night!

#3146 AN INVITATION TO SIN
Sicily's Corretti Dynasty
Sarah Morgan
Taylor Carmichael holds one thing precious: the reputation she's spent years rebuilding. Then one encounter with Corretti lothario Luca, a bottle of chilled champagne and a skin-tight dress and everything falls apart.

#3147 HIS FINAL BARGAIN
Melanie Milburne
Eliza Lincoln is stunned to find Leo Valente at her door; four years ago his passionate embrace was a brief taste of freedom from her suffocating engagement. Now he's back, and he has a proposition he knows Eliza can't refuse....

#3148 FORGIVEN BUT NOT FORGOTTEN?
Abby Green
Andreas Xenakis waited years to get his revenge on the DePiero family and now he finally has destitute heiress Siena at his mercy. But after just one night together everything Andreas believed about poor little rich girl Siena is shattered.

You can find more information on upcoming Harlequin® titles, free excerpts and more at www.Harlequin.com.

HPCNM0513RA

#3149 DIAMOND IN THE DESERT
Susan Stephens

With the future of the Skavanga diamond mine in jeopardy, heiress Britt Skavanga needs an injection of cash—fast. She finds it in the mysterious Arabian investor known only as *Emir*...but his exacting fee is not financial!

#3150 A GREEK ESCAPE
Elizabeth Power

Jilted by her cheating boyfriend, her self-esteem in tatters, Kayla Young escapes to an isolated Greek island. But the last thing she wants is to have to share her precious paradise with the mysterious, arrogant Leonidas Vassalio.

#3151 A THRONE FOR THE TAKING
Royal & Ruthless
Kate Walker

Betrayed by those she loves, Honoria Escalona must face the only man capable of bringing stability to the kingdom of Mecjoria. But Alexei Sarova's past has changed him into someone she hardly knows, and his help comes with a price....

#3152 PRINCESS IN THE IRON MASK
Victoria Parker

Dispatched by the king to retrieve his headstrong daughter, Lucas Garcia thought this was just another day at the office. That's before he meets Princess Claudine, who's adamant that returning to her father's kingdom is never going to happen!

HPCNM0513RB

REQUEST YOUR FREE BOOKS!

2 FREE NOVELS PLUS
2 FREE GIFTS!

PASSION
GUARANTEED
SEDUCTION

SPECIAL EXCERPT FROM

H HARLEQUIN®
™

Presents

Dispatched by the king to retrieve his headstrong daughter, Lucas Garcia thought this was just another day at the office…until he meets Princess Claudine Verbault.

Enjoy a sneak preview of PRINCESS IN THE IRON MASK by debut author Victoria Parker.

* * *

"You barge into my life and proceed to conduct some sort of military operation. And now you're going on like an interfering, dictatorial knave!"

Suddenly Lucas stopped and turned on his heels to face her. "Do you have an aversion to authority, Claudia? Is that what this is? You don't like being told what to do?"

The gray silken weave of his tailored suit began to turn black as the rain seeped through his clothing. His overlong hair was already dripping and plastered to his smooth forehead and the high slash of his cheekbones. And the sight of him, wet and disheveled, flooded her with heat. Like this he was far more powerful and dangerous to her equilibrium. He looked gloriously untamed.

"No, actually, I don't. Do you think it's right to force someone against their every wish? To blackmail in order to do your job?" Something dark flashed in his eyes, but she was too far gone to care. "And because I dare to put up some sort of fight, you deem me selfish and irresponsible. Do you have any feelings?"

"I am not paid to feel," he ground out, taking a step closer toward her.

"It's a good job, 'cos you'd be broke," she replied, taking a step back.

Lucas pinched the bridge of his nose with his thumb and forefinger. "You're the most provoking woman I have ever met."

A mere two feet away, Claudia could feel the heat radiating from his broad torso. Oh God, she had to get away from him before she did something seriously stupid. Like smooth her hands up his soaked shirt. "You know what, Lucas? I'm staying here."

Before he could say another word, she bolted sideways. Only to be blocked by a one-arm barricade.

"Over my dead body," he growled, corralling her back toward the car.

* * *

Find out who will win the battle of wills in
PRINCESS IN THE IRON MASK by Victoria Parker,
available May 21, 2013.

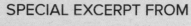
The more powerful the family...the darker the secrets....

Read on for an exclusive sneak peek from
AN INVITATION TO SIN by USA TODAY bestselling
author Sarah Morgan, book #2 in the epic new miniseries
SICILY'S CORRETTI DYNASTY.

* * *

TAYLOR reminded herself that Luca Corretti was probably the most dangerous man she could possibly have found herself with. "I thought you were trying to behave yourself."

"This is me behaving myself." He took another mouthful of champagne, and she laughed in spite of herself, sensing a kindred spirit. A part of her long buried stirred to life.

"So both of us are making a superhuman effort to behave. What's your excuse?"

"I have to prove myself capable of taking charge of the family business." Underneath the light, careless tone there was an edge of steel and it surprised her. She didn't associate him with responsibility.

That thought was followed instantaneously by guilt. She was judging him, just as others judged her and she was better than that.

"But you turned the House of Corretti around."

"I have a flare for figures."

"Especially when those figures belong to models?"

He laughed. "Something like that."

"But why do you want to meddle in other parts of the business?"

"Sibling rivalry."

"But you're all members of the same family. Surely that qualifies you for a seat on the board."

"The qualifications for a seat on the board seem to be old age and sexual inactivity." He suppressed a yawn. "I suppose that's why they call it a 'bored.' I have a feeling that whatever I do, I will always be in the wrong."

Taylor felt a flicker of sympathy. "I know that feeling."

"I'm sure you do. You, Taylor Carmichael, are one big walking wrong." His gaze lingered on her mouth. "So tell me what else is on your list of banned substances."

"Men like you."

"Is that right?" Somehow, without her even noticing how he'd done it, he'd moved closer to her. His dark head was between her and the sun and all she could see were those wicked eyes tempting her toward the dark side.

"What are you doing?"

"Testing a theory." His mouth moved closer to hers, and suddenly she struggled to breathe.

"What theory?"

"I want to know whether two wrongs make a right." His smile was the last thing she saw before he kissed her.

* * *

Find out if sinfully attractive Luca's theory proves to be right in AN INVITATION TO SIN by Sarah Morgan. Available May 21, 2013, wherever books are sold!